Dating4 Demons

Dating 4 Demons

Serena Robar

BERKLEY JAM, NEW YORK

THE BERKLEY PUBLISHING GROUP
Published by the Penguin Group
Penguin Group (USA) Inc.
375 Hudson Street, New York, New York 10014, USA
Penguin Group (Canada), 90 Eglinton Avenue East, Suite 700, Toronto, Ontario M4P 2Y3, Canada
(a division of Pearson Penguin Canada Inc.)
Penguin Books Ltd., 80 Strand, London WC2R 0RL, England
Penguin Group Ireland, 25 St. Stephen's Green, Dublin 2, Ireland (a division of Penguin Books Ltd.)
Penguin Group (Australia), 250 Camberwell Road, Camberwell, Victoria 3124, Australia
(a division of Pearson Australia Group Pty. Ltd.)
Penguin Books India Pvt. Ltd., 11 Community Centre, Panchsheel Park, New Delhi—110 017, India
Penguin Group (NZ), 67 Apollo Drive, Rosedale, North Shore 0745, Auckland, New Zealand
(a division of Pearson New Zealand Ltd.)
Penguin Books (South Africa) (Pty.) Ltd., 24 Sturdee Avenue, Rosebank, Johannesburg 2196,
South Africa

Penguin Books Ltd., Registered Offices: 80 Strand, London WC2R 0RL, England

This book is an original publication of The Berkley Publishing Group.

This is a work of fiction. Names, characters, places, and incidents either are the product of the author's imagination or are used fictitiously, and any resemblance to actual persons, living or dead, business establishments, events, or locales is entirely coincidental. The publisher does not have any control over and does not assume any responsibility for author or third-party websites or their content.

PRINTING HISTORY
Berkley JAM trade paperback edition / May 2007

Library of Congress Cataloging-in-Publication Data

Robar, Serena.
  Dating4demons / Serena Robar.—Berkley Jam trade paperback ed.
    p. cm.
  Summary: As Colby, the Protector of the half-blood vampires, continues to fight off full-bloods, take care of her sorority sisters, keep up with coursework, and decipher the prophesy that claims she will bring about the end of the world, her best friend, Piper, stakes a demon zombie and learns she is a demon slayer.
  ISBN 978-0-425-21514-2
  [1. Vampires—Fiction. 2. Demoniac possession—Fiction. 3. Dating (Social customs)—Fiction. 4. Best friends—Fiction. 5. Friendship—Fiction. 6. Universities and colleges—Fiction. 7. Horror stories.] I. Title. II. Title: Dating 4 demons. III. Title: Dating for demons.

  PZ7.R5312Dat 2007
  [Fic]—dc22

                                                                              2007000316

PRINTED IN THE UNITED STATES OF AMERICA

10 9 8 7 6 5 4 3 2 1

This book is dedicated to my daughter, Taylor Lynn—and I promise to use only the juiciest stories from your adolescence for my books. Mwuahahahahahaha!

Acknowledgments

Without my husband, Jason, this book would still be sitting in my head and nowhere near book form. I thank you for watching the kids, eating TV dinners and generally being neglected while I wrote.

As always, thanks for the support of The Tiaras: Christina Arbini, Erin Eisenberg, Kelli Estes and Shannon McKelden.

And a special thanks to Leis Pederson, who kicked my butt when I needed to make deadline.

Colby Blanchard
Undead Living 102
Being Undead
Short Essay

Being Undead: What It Means to Me

In the fall of my senior year of high school, I walked home after a football game, alone. I was attacked by a rogue vampire who changed me into a vampire. I quickly discovered (after a visit from some Vampire Investigators) that I was Undead without a license—and not even a full-blood vampire, only a half-blood. Normally, I would have been destroyed, but I provided a pretty compelling argument. In the end, I managed to get a license, emancipate other half-bloods and was given a job as their Protector. But full-bloods still don't like us. At all.

Why? Well, it appears I am prophesied in some ancient texts to bring about the end of the world.

> *This time the mixed blood will rise,*
> *The One who is Undead but Alive,*

Who is pure but not whole,
And they will bring forth the beginning of the end.

So, what's being Undead mean to me? It means I have no time. Since full-bloods don't like me, they all want to kill me so I'm constantly dodging stakes and swords, and I never have time to finish my assignments. Which is why this essay is late.

One

COLBY

found it hard to believe that such a big guy was even attempting to look inconspicuous while obviously following me, but there he was, *again*. This time he was feigning interest in some shades while I cruised the Sunglass Hut. He was handsome in a bad boy, no, scratch that, in a *Piper* sort of way. I giggled at the thought. My best friend, Piper, would love the seriously dark vibe this guy was emitting. It would appeal to her whole, I'm-not-Goth-I'm-alternative persona.

I took a deep breath once more and relaxed. He wasn't a vampire at least. Of that I was sure. And he smelled like oatmeal raisin cookies with a hint of cinnamon. It was my experience (admittedly limited) that men who smelled like cookies were probably not evil. Yeah, it was pigeonholing an entire olfactory type but hey, stereotypes exist for a reason, you know.

He might not have been a vampire, but that didn't mean I shouldn't be cautious. It seemed like every other night I was being attacked by some ancient vampire who followed the Prophesy. Occasionally they even brought a human pet or two with them. They believed Colby Blanchard (that would be me) was the one who would bring about the end of their existence as we knew it. Tell a friend. Film at eleven. Sheesh, start a small revolution by emancipating half-blood vampires, and suddenly everyone thinks you're up to no good. It wasn't my fault that half-bloods were considered an abomination by all. But not anymore. I was a half-blood and proud of it. No one who dressed as well as I did was an abomination. Period.

No, this guy wasn't a vampire and I thought it unlikely he was a pet. Pets tended to be very robotic and couldn't think for themselves. They were under a spell and looked spaced-out all the time. Nope, this guy could never be anyone's pet.

Maybe he was just shy and wanted to meet me? Probably. I mean, I looked pretty hot today with my spray-on tan and Psi Phi tank top. Sure, it was the middle of April and still a bit chilly for the Northwest, but when you're dead, er, Undead, a couple degrees didn't matter much. Call it a perk, if you will.

I made my way upstairs to the food court. I wanted Piper to meet me before the sun went down, but no, she was doing some homework and couldn't break away until the evening. As a half-blood, I was able to walk around during the day. Sure, I had to wear lotion with an SPF of about a gazillion but I didn't mind.

I wasn't thrilled to meet Piper after dark, though. What with all the kill-the-prophet-chick stuff going on. I mean, putting your best friend in danger meant she wouldn't be your best friend for long. That was unacceptable. I needed Piper. I needed her like I needed sunlight—wait a minute, I didn't actually need sunlight and should really avoid it. Okay then, I needed her like I needed food. Hmm. I didn't need food either. Well, I needed Piper and I really shouldn't have to justify keeping my friends safe.

I reached the third floor and found her standing in line at Hot Dog on a Stick. I picked out a table and waited for her, shaking my head when I saw what she was wearing. Why, oh why did she have the fashion sense of a transient?

She sported Lucky jeans with a white leather belt, ritually studded with metal brads in a uniform pattern. She'd paired a long-sleeve black mesh shirt, ripped at the collarbone and along one elbow, over a fitted burgundy tank with a black bra. Piper was short, around five-four, and curvy. That was to say she had a small waist, huge boobs and rounded bottom. She was wearing black Converse high-tops, natch. We wouldn't want to spread our wings and wear another pair of shoes or anything.

Still, with her shoulder-length, jet-black hair with burgundy streaks and her fondness for eyeliner, she had a style all her own. Coupled with a row of earrings and pierced nose, she was exotic, in a don't-sit-next-to-me-on-the-bus sort of way.

"Dew?" I inquired as she sipped some liquid through a straw. Piper lived on Mountain Dew.

"Nope, cherry lemonade."

I made a gagging sound in the back of my throat. Piper sure loved syrupy sweet drinks. And apparently, fried food on a stick. She'd bought a corndog as well, then smothered it in mustard. I shuddered.

"Did you drag me all the way to the mall to insult my taste in drinks or did you have a real reason for meeting here?"

She plopped down next to me, maneuvering her drink, plate and the monster-size tote bag at her side.

"Bag lady," I muttered under my breath.

"I heard that, and for your information, I have a present for you in this bag," Piper said, not bothering to look up from her task of finding a portion of floor that was not too sticky to deposit her tote.

"A present? For me?"

"Yep. Cyrus made a bunch of wooden stakes for you. Thought you should keep them around the House and stuff. I just saw him."

"You went to training?" I was incredulous. Getting Piper to go to self-defense practice was like pulling teeth. I insisted the House attend training with Cyrus but Piper always had other things to do.

She ignored my comment and reiterated, "So, we're at the mall, why?"

"Do I need a reason to hang at the mall with my best friend?" I said brightly.

Piper was instantly suspicious. I guess I said it a little too brightly.

"What's wrong?"

"What do you mean 'What's wrong?' Can't we get together outside the House for a little girl time at the mall without something being wrong?"

Piper just stared at me.

"Yeah, okay. Well, I was wondering if you'd made any progress on deciphering that stupid Prophesy yet." I hated to sound needy but I was kind of getting tired of being jumped every time I strolled around the park looking for a little midnight snack.

"Were you attacked again?" Piper asked, concern replacing her normal sarcastic tone.

"Aw, shucks, Piper. Are you worried about me?" I fluttered my eyelashes at her. Piper snorted.

"If you'd quit dressing like a streetwalker, the attacks would stop."

I blinked once. Twice. Not sure if I heard her correctly. She laughed at my expression, no longer able to hold a straight face.

"Oh hardy, har, har." My voice dripped acid.

"Don't you think if I found the true meaning of the Prophesy, I would have called you right away?" she questioned after her laughter died down.

"Yeah, I'm just getting tired of playing dodge the stake and last night, well"—I shook my head in remembrance—"I was dodging a sword. A freakin' *sword*, Piper. I mean, who walks around campus waving a sword without getting busted by campus security?"

Piper sat up straighter and demanded, "Did you tell Thomas?"

I nibbled on my lower lip wondering how to answer that one. "I would have told Thomas," I ventured slowly, "but he has a lot going on right now with all the rogue vampires attacking people and stuff."

Thomas was my Vampire Investigator boyfriend and a full-blood. He'd helped me when I was first changed and we'd grown pretty close in the last year. Yet lately, well . . . I didn't want to burden Piper about Thomas's weird loner behavior. I mean, he was working his cute butt off nightly trying to keep the public safe from vampires who were freaking out about the stupid Prophesy that had everyone thinking I was going to destroy their existence—Puh-lease, like I would if I could—but I was a big girl now. I was the half-blood Protector, for goodness' sake.

"It's Thomas's job to protect the people and get the bad vampires. He can handle it. He would want to know, Colby."

She was right, of course. He *would* want to know, but I felt bad adding to his workload. He was having nightmares when he slept and they were really unnerving. I didn't even like to cuddle next to him anymore because they bothered me so much; and once, well, once he'd swung out as though he were fighting some unknown foe and knocked me right out of the bed. When I woke him he didn't remember a thing. He claimed he wasn't having them anymore but the dark circles under his eyes told me another story. He wanted to protect me as much as I wanted to protect him. Boy, did we have control issues or what?

"Yeah, I know. I plan to tell him. I just hoped I could add good news with the bad like, I was attacked with a sword last night but Piper figured out the Prophesy so hey, there won't be any more pin-the-sword-through-the-Colby night games."

"Sorry to disappoint," Piper said, rolling her corndog around in the mustard, trying to gob on more—if that was even possible.

"You're gonna get a stomachache," I warned as she took a bite.

"You're just jealous because I can eat real food," she gloated.

"You know, a true friend wouldn't rub that in and probably wouldn't even eat in front of me." I pouted prettily.

She took another bite and chewed with her mouth open, showing me everything I was missing.

"Ew, gross!"

She smacked her lips after swallowing and smiled smugly.

"Fine, next time I'm hungry, I'll feed in front of you." It was an empty threat. I wasn't about to let Piper watch me suck down a pint of O negative from some unsuspecting victim. Piper had a very weak stomach.

Ignoring me, she asked, "How is Aunt Chloe doing?"

I rolled my eyes in answer. Aunt Chloe was actually my great-great-aunt but everyone just called her "Aunt Chloe." She used to be a nurse during World War II and the Korean War. She was feisty and opinionated and was currently acting as the Psi Phi House's sorority mother.

"It's only temporary. A big façade, actually. I can't believe the administration threatened to revoke our sorority status because we didn't have a live-in housemother. Sheesh. I'm glad Aunt Chloe is helping us out, but I think she misses her friends at Providence Point, and frankly, she's getting down-right bossy."

Aunt Chloe normally lived in an upscale retirement community on the Eastside, but when I needed a housemother ASAP, she packed her bags and moved in. All without my consent, might I add. In theory, it was a good fit. She knew I was Undead and knew that all the girls at Psi Phi House were half-bloods as well. She wasn't even squeamish about sleeping in the same room where we found a murdered half-blood hidden in a trunk last year.

"Pish posh," she'd said when I objected to her sleeping there. "There isn't a day gone by I don't see an ambulance picking up a body somewhere in Providence Point. People die, Colby. That's part of the cycle. Nothing to be scared of." And that was basically Aunt Chloe in a nutshell. She was one tough ol' bird.

"Bossy? How?" Piper wanted to know.

"Well, first of all she gave us all household chores and

harps on us constantly to get them done. She even made us a chart! She decided it was much too important to trust us to make our own study times, so she instituted set Quiet Time sessions—and attendance is mandatory. She claims the girls lack discipline and need to understand the importance of passing their Undead courses. Seems to me everyone understands if they don't pass the course, they don't get a vampire license; without that, they'll be relieved of their Undead status. You know." I made a swift cutting motion across my neck to emphasize my point. "They all get how important the classes are to their existence."

"Sounds like she's just trying to help," Piper noted.

"Tell that to Sage. Aunt Chloe put her on a diet."

Piper looked shocked, "How do you put a vampire on a diet? And for that matter, why put her on a diet? You guys stay the same after you die, right?"

"Only full-bloods apparently. Sage, for some weird reason, is able to consume milk products. And she loves shakes. Has them all the time. She is forever walking to the Starbucks and getting a Frappuccino after her nightly feeding. Anyway, we all noticed she had to go out and buy new clothes, 'cause her other ones were too tight. Her face was getting rounder and finally Aunt Chloe told her she was getting fat. I mean right to her face she said, 'Sage, you're getting fat. I'm putting you on a diet.'"

Piper made a noise somewhere between a gasp of dismay and a chortle of laughter.

"I know," I agreed with the sentiment behind the sound, "I couldn't believe it either. Sage got all flustered and embarrassed but Aunt Chloe didn't relent. She made Sage a chart as well, to keep count of her daily feeding and shake intake."

"That's awful."

I shrugged. "I'd rather be on the diet chart than the boy chart."

"I'm almost afraid to ask what the boy chart is," Piper said.

I smirked at her. "Remember last fall how our football team was being affected by a strange illness that was making them all weak and light-headed?"

Piper shook her head. "Vaguely."

"It seemed the basketball team was struck with the same mysterious illness. The guys were passing out in practice and no one, not even the coaches or the team doctors, could figure out why. But Aunt Chloe did."

"How?"

"She's always listening to us. One day the girls were talking about their nightly feedings and who was dating who and before I know it, she announced the boy chart. She told us each time we feed from an athlete, we put their name under our column and no one can feed on the same athlete for at least two weeks. Several of the gals have a thing for jocks and they were hooking up and feeding on the same guys. These guys were literally being sucked dry by Psi Phi House."

Piper let out a bark of laughter, then clamped a hand over

her mouth when everyone in the food court turned to stare. She shook with the effort to hold it in, but couldn't seem to stop giggling.

"Sure, laugh it up. It was pretty shocking for the girls to see their favorite flavor on another girl's column. I thought Angie was going to stake one of the new girls, Manda, after seeing three of her favorite treats under her name."

"Are you on the 'ho chart?" Piper asked suddenly.

"It's called the *boy* chart," I corrected primly. "And no, I am not. I have Thomas and I never feed on the same person twice."

I didn't elaborate on the fact that Thomas had such rich blood that I could feed on him and not need to eat for the rest of the day, and vice versa. Anyway, feeding with Thomas was not like feeding on a stranger. It had an entirely different effect on me—one I wasn't about to share with Piper.

"Yeah, I bet." She smirked at me but I didn't rise to the bait.

"So, back to the Prophesy. How's progress?" I felt it was prudent to change the subject or Piper would figure out feeding was a passionate pastime between Thomas and myself. I was relieved when she let it go.

"Actually, I have a couple of ideas on that front. How do we know that the Prophesy was translated properly? I want to double-check the scripts we have with the original and then find a professional who can translate them again. So much can get lost in a translation, nuances can be misinterpreted. Maybe it's not as bad as we think."

"That's it? All you've got is wishful thinking?" I tried not to sound annoyed, but hoping the Prophesy was somehow mistranslated seemed like a long shot at best.

Piper remained stubborn. "I need to know the information we have is accurate. I don't know the history, the context or the myths surrounding this stupid thing, so I think it's prudent to make sure what we have is solid."

I threw my hands up in surrender. "Okay, okay. You win. I'm sorry. I'm a little on edge, ya know? Thomas mentioned something about scripts being transported to the vampire library. Maybe I can get a peek at them. I can get you a copy of the text in its original language, if that helps."

"Why can't I go with you?"

"They are never going to let you in the library, much less nose around in the private collections," I told her.

"Is it because of the whole 'I breathe, therefore I live' thing?" Piper quipped

"Something like that. Tell me what to look for and I'll try to get a look at them."

"Try? You mean you don't know if you can see the private stuff either?"

"The librarian and I don't really see eye to eye." I reluctantly admitted, "I don't think she likes me."

"Imagine that," Piper said dryly. "A full-blood who doesn't like the half-blood Protector. Shocker."

I nodded. "Hard to believe that I'm not loved and adored

by the entire full-blood population, but there you go. I'll see if Mr. Holloway can get me access."

Mr. Holloway was a member of the Vampire Tribunal. He was one of the three head honcho Undead. I kind of kept a dark secret of his so he's willing to do stuff for me.

"Failing that, I guess I pay a little visit during the day."

"You mean break in?" Piper clarified.

"Jeez, when you put it like that it sounds so sordid, Piper," I complained. She laughed at me.

"Fine, but I get to be Bonnie. You're Clyde," she teased.

"You don't get to go. Too dangerous."

"What do you mean, 'too dangerous'? We go during the day when all the vampires can't go out. How dangerous is that?" She was peeved.

"Listen, Piper, it's way too risky for you to go. Not gonna happen."

My declaration was met with silence, which was so unlike Piper. I noticed her looking over my shoulder, mouth forming a small O of surprise. It didn't take a rocket scientist to figure out my stalker had stepped out of the shadows. And I was so right, he was definitely Piper's type, if the look on her face was any indication.

TWO

PIPER

I have to admit, when I first saw the guy walking through the food court, I felt a bolt of electricity surge through me. And it's not like I, Piper Prescott, feel hottie volts race through my body on a regular basis. As a matter of fact, I couldn't remember ever feeling this way before. I mean, when this guy looked at me, it was like he looked at *me*. Past the exterior I chose to show the world, past the attitude, past it all. He could really see me, you know? The only other person who truly saw me, in my opinion, was Colby and let's face it, chick factor aside, she is totally not my type.

However, if the walking rebel with long black hair sweeping his broad shoulders would just, oh yeah, rake his fingers through that single layer of inky darkness, I might swoon. Well, at least tremble a little on the inside, playing it oh-so-cool on the outside. The guy was yum-my.

I looked at Colby and immediately noted the knowing

smirk on her face. Sure, things like this were easy for her. She could always have her pick of guys. Even Aidan, her last flavor of the month before Thomas, had been an easy conquest at several parties. Let's face facts here: Colby hadn't been the deepest of chicks in those days. Actually, she was a downright vapid twit most of the time. But when she was attacked and changed into a half-vampire, the old Colby reemerged fighting. It took real guts to take on the Vampire Council and fight for her life. But to throw the dice and go all or nothing—emancipating all half-bloods instead of just thinking about herself—was totally ballsy. That's why we were best friends.

And since we were best friends, she obviously knew I liked what I saw.

"Let me guess?" she asked drily. "Tall, dark and menacing in a very sexy sort of way just crossed the food court, right?"

"Who is that guy?" I asked breathlessly.

Colby peeked over her shoulder toward the general direction of my salivating stare and caught him looking at us with an unfathomable expression. Suddenly, she moved her chair so that she sat between him and me, effectively blocking my view.

"Hey!" I complained.

"Sorry." She sounded anything but. "Don't know who he is, but I can tell he's trouble."

Sure, she was just trying to protect me from possible harm, but this was just the kind of guy I wouldn't mind being in a dangerous position with. I gave a dramatic sigh as she lifted my tote of stakes from the floor.

"I like trouble." I pouted childishly, but allowed her to keep a defensive stance between us.

"Yeah." Colby snorted knowingly. "I know exactly what kind of trouble you like and that's why I'm standing between it and you."

She stood up and I chuckled, then gasped in pain.

"What's wrong?" she asked, bending over to assist me.

I took a deep breath and tried to straighten up.

Is it that time of the month already?

"Ever have those killer cramps that make you wonder why giving birth was ever considered a blessing for women?"

"Are you telling me that cry of pain was from PMS?" Colby asked, astonished.

I stood up, indignant. "You know, not all of us get the crap knocked out of us on a daily basis and are numb to pain. Some of us are actually delicate flowers, you big oaf."

She laughed at me and looped my arm through hers as we made our way toward the escalators. I took a quick glimpse around the food court and discovered my new infatuation had vanished. There were a couple of disheveled-looking men close to the elevators who seemed to be taking a particular interest in us as we made our exit but since they didn't follow, I wasn't too concerned. Colby and I always turned heads when we were out. At least, Colby always turned heads.

I didn't consider myself a ravishing beauty, but our styles were so different, we just didn't look like we belonged together.

We took the escalator down several floors, and then I directed Colby toward the door leading to the parking garage.

"I parked down a floor."

I was annoyed I wouldn't have access to forbidden vampire scripts. It seemed so unfair that she needed my help but would only let me do so much. I would never tell Colby this, but secretly I loved investigating the ancient prophesies. Unlike the female Terminator next to me, I didn't care for the physical side of her Protector role. She forced me to take self-defense classes with the rest of the half-bloods so I would be as safe as possible, but I fought her tooth and nail about attending regularly.

It wasn't that I was a wuss or anything. The truth of the matter is, I could trash-talk with the best of them; usually, that was enough. I don't think I've ever really had to walk the walk, ya know what I mean?

Colby and I looked like our exact opposites in so many ways. I might look all tough and stuff but I had a weak stomach and was really more of the damsel in distress type. Which is really quite funny when you think about it. I mean, most people would assume Colby needed protection, not me.

As a matter of fact, the last time I had a tussle with a real vampire, I froze and—this is so embarrassing to admit—I actually *curled into a fetal position on the grass*. Colby claimed all's well that ends well because she used me to trip the bad guy onto a picket fence and save the day. Can you believe she took advantage of me like that? Forget that I was frozen with fear. She's such an opportunist when the situation calls for it.

"Some of the lights are out on this level," Colby mentioned, trying to find my car in the dimness.

"I'm over there." I pointed to the second row when I felt a knifelike pain shoot through my stomach again. I cried out in pain and doubled over. Colby reacted quicker than my eyes could follow, bending and catching me before I hit the cement floor. At the same moment we both heard a *ku-thunk* of something breaking against the pillar behind her. Before I knew what was happening, she catapulted both of us behind the closest vehicle.

Luckily it was a Honda Odyssey and we had room to maneuver.

"Are you hurt?" she demanded, checking my body for injuries.

I gasped again, the stabbing pain causing me to clutch my stomach, and asked through clenched teeth, "What the hell was that?"

She quickly peeked through the van's windows out into the parking garage, trying to identify the whereabouts of our attacker.

"Arrow," she said grimly.

"Arrow?" I replied in a bit of a panicked tone. "Someone is shooting at us with freakin' arrows?"

This was no time for cramps so I took a deep breath and tried balancing on the balls of my feet. When I felt steady I looked around as well.

"Can you run?" she asked me uncertainly. As though I could read her mind, I realized she had no idea what we were facing; and if I couldn't make a run for it, she wasn't sure she could protect me. It was just the sort of catalyst I needed.

"I can run." I was grim but determined.

She nodded in agreement. "Okay. When I tell you to, I want you to run back the way we came. We're pretty close to the door. Run into the crowds. They won't come after you with a lot of people around."

"What are you going to do?" I asked anxiously.

"I'm going to try and slow them down, then I'll join . . ."

"Protector! Come out, come out where ever you are!" A singsong voice broke the relative silence of the parking garage.

"We have you surrounded," the mysterious voice assured us. I took a quick look toward my planned emergency exit and confirmed we were, indeed, surrounded. One of the disheveled men I'd noticed by the elevator in the food court was hanging out by the door, his eyes searching the darkness for his prey.

"Colby?" I questioned softy, totally out of my element. You see, this was her department. She was forever getting attacked by vampires who don't like her because she's a half-blood. I wasn't usually part of the equation—and frankly, I preferred it that way.

"You stay here. When I tell you to run, you do it. No questions asked. Got it?" Colby looked self-assured and confident, so I bobbed my head up and down in affirmation. She had a plan, which had to be better than my plan since my plan consisted of cowering by the tires. When she started to move, I grabbed her arm and pulled my bag from my shoulder. I couldn't believe I'd forgotten I had goodies for just this sort of occasion.

She grinned cockily and I returned the smile after she plucked the biggest stake out of my tote. I'd written "Stake-o-matic" on them as a joke. It didn't seem as funny now that I was going to witness her using them.

She put a hand on my shoulder and gave it a small, comforting pat before quickly moving past several parked cars and emerging far away from our hiding spot. You have no idea how happy I was that it was nighttime and she was at full Undead power. Part of the whole half-blood gig was that many only possessed a few vampire powers and then maybe just the watered-down version. Colby was very kick-ass when it was nighttime. Don't ask me why, it was what it was.

"Dude!" I heard her taunt as she stepped out between cars a good ways from where she started. "What kind of pansy uses arrows on a girl? Are you afraid the big, bad Protector is gonna kick your butt in front of all your little friends?"

We seriously needed to work on her trash-talking.

From my position I could identify four of the five guys from the food court. I wasn't sure where the last guy was, which made me nervous.

I yelped when Colby jumped onto the closest car as an arrow pierced the space she'd occupied only a moment before. She jumped from car to car, going right for mystery man number five as he fired another bolt from his crossbow. Colby dodged, *Matrix* style, by doing a truly spectacular vault/cartwheel thingy onto the car closest to the creep. I cheered in my head when she landed perfectly. Her attacker didn't even have time to reload and threw his weapon at her instead.

She caught it in the shoulder but it barely slowed her down, because she was already delivering a fierce kick to his chin, practically snapping his head off. She finished the job with her stake and I realized I had a serious girl crush on my best friend. I mean, who wouldn't be part of the Colby fan club after seeing her fight?

She'd nailed him in the chest and I was surprised to see a white mist escape the puncture with a hiss. It rose over the body, seemed to suspend in midair for a moment and then dissipate.

WTF? This didn't happen the last time I'd witnessed a vampire wasting. True, I'd only seen one and this was far from Colby's first whacking but she'd never mentioned the mist before. The look on her face led me to believe it was her first time as well.

I glanced at the door; the guy guarding it was running toward the fight. I could make my escape now but I hesitated. It was obvious Colby was up against something she hadn't expected and now she had four of them teaming up on her. She neatly staked a second one that exploded a pus that caused her to jump back.

Sure, killing vamps was never pretty but they usually just dissolve nicely into a puddle of goo. At least, that was my limited experience. This whole smelly, oozy thing was new to me. And I had to say, I didn't like it at all. I had a feeling if any of it got on Colby's shoes, she would go medieval. Colby had a thing for shoes, don't ask me why.

Number Three grabbed her from behind and Number Four punched her in the face. I debated running to the door. Could I really leave her now? She was getting punched in the face. But besides pissing her off, punching her in the face wasn't going to stop her.

Then she did something so shocking, she actually shrieked. She reached back behind her for Number Three, grabbed his head and pulled, hard. I expected him to come flying over her shoulder into Number Four and I think she must have as well. To my shock and dismay, his head detached from his body and now Colby was holding it upside down against her chest.

She tossed it to Number Four; the surprised look on his face was pretty classic. He threw it back and before I knew it they were playing a game of hot potato with this guy's noggin. The fifth guy arrived in time to slap the head out of Colby's hand and knock her to the ground with a single punch. He was huge and ugly and very, very angry.

I watched him kick her twice as she yelled for me to run. But I couldn't just leave even though I really wanted to do just that: run far and wide. Colby was taking a serious beating. So instead I moved toward the battle, armed with a stake from my tote. I know, I am too stupid to be allowed to live, but I had to try to help her.

As I approached, Colby grabbed the smaller of the two guys and used him as a shield when the big one produced a wicked-looking blade. It was bigger than a knife but smaller than a sword. Who did this guy think he was, anyway, Captain Jack Sparrow?

The big guy effectively slashed his partner to ribbons as Colby dodged his slicing and dicing action. I was whimpering when I realized she had nothing left to use as a shield, and then Colby slipped on the oozy mess and went down on one knee, hard. I heard the crack her kneecap made from my hiding place.

Her face was contorted with pain and she was defenseless. The big guy brought up his sword and a power that I couldn't begin to describe filled me. I leapt forward, stake in hand, poised for action when I heard the man say to Colby, "It's time to go."

With a force I didn't know I possessed, I rammed the pointed wood into his back, between the ribs and into his heart. "After you," I gasped.

The stench of spoiled milk filled the air as he sank to the ground, a white mist pouring from his back.

As the attacker sank between us, Colby's expression was one of amazement and shock. Did she really think I would leave her to die? Gee, thanks a lot.

"You saved me," she whispered, clearly flabbergasted at the turn of events.

"Duh," I rallied with sarcasm after Colby stated the obvious.

Her expression changed from one of shock to new respect and not a little bit of awe. I felt like an all-avenging angel with my slimy stake and bubbly bad guy decomposing at my feet. The adrenaline rush quickly left me as the overwhelming stench of spoiled dairy products invaded my senses. I dropped the stake to cover my mouth. I felt the corndog rise in my throat as a sexy, deep voice asked, "Are you okay? Can I help?"

My hottie from the mall had arrived just in time to wear my mustard-laden dinner on his biker boots.

Three

COLBY

"Piper, you're amazing!" I praised, completely ignoring my would-be stalker. He wasn't a vampire and hadn't jumped in to finish us off. At this point he wasn't an immediate threat.

"I'm so sorry." Piper moaned, wiping her mouth with the torn sleeve of her shirt.

"Uh, that's okay. Are you sick? What happened?" the guy asked her, shaking the vomit from his boots, one foot at a time.

I took that moment to attempt some damage control. It was time to determine what he saw and what he knew.

"What do you think happened here?" I asked shrewdly. "Some punk kids threw spoiled dairy products everywhere, making my friend ill and causing me to fall and hurt myself in the process." It was the lamest, sorriest tale I had ever told and seriously, I'd told some whoppers in my day.

"Ri-ght." He nodded slowly, looking around at the chaos and sounding not a little unlike Dr. Evil in his skepticism.

I decided lying might not fly so I turned into an invalid. People rarely demanded answers right away from an injured girl.

"A little help here?" I ventured, going from agitated liar to weak-kneed female.

"Oh, Colby. Are you okay?" Piper rushed to my side and I rolled my eyes at her. She of all people couldn't be falling for my act, could she?

"I've been better. And what happened to the plan, Piper?" I accepted the offer of help and leaned against her, trying to flex my leg. I winced in pain (only slightly exaggerating) as it made a popping noise when I straightened it.

"Is your kneecap broken?" he asked incredulously.

I waved his concern aside. "No, no. Old cheerleading injury. I'm double-jointed and the knee pops out sometimes."

I smiled brightly in his direction, looking directly into his eyes, and saw his body relax. I channeled all my Undead mojo into the stare and could practically hear him thinking, *Of course. That's it. Nothing to worry about there. She must have tripped. But now she is perfectly fine.*

"Stop it, Colby," Piper demanded, glaring at me. The guy broke eye contact and looked back toward her, visibly tensing once he was no longer caught by the power of my gaze. *Damn it, Piper!*

"She slipped on this *goo* and went down hard. Can you help me get her to my car?" And then Piper actually fluttered her eyelashes at him. She wouldn't let me use my hypnotic powers but it was fine and dandy to use her feminine wiles? And since when did Piper use feminine wiles anyway? This evening was getting weirder and weirder.

I looked at him and asked bluntly, "Where did you come from?"

He swept me up into his arms in one motion. "I noticed you on the floor when I was walking to my bike and thought you were hurt. My name's Hunter, by the way."

He carried me easily; I had to admit it was impressive how Piper barfing on his boots hadn't fazed him and how carrying a total stranger to her car was no big deal. And really, what gal isn't a little enthralled when a man can sweep her up in his arms so effortlessly? That's why firefighters are such popular fantasy fodder. This guy was definitely hot on so many levels, but I sensed he could be dangerous as well.

"I'm Colby and this is Piper."

He smiled at Piper, flashing a dimple in his left cheek, and I could practically hear her purr. It was disgusting. And sadly, I felt a little purr coming on myself when I felt his chest muscles ripple as he carefully lowered me to the ground so I could get in the backseat of Piper's car.

I love my boyfriend, who is one fine specimen of manliness, but this Hunter was built like a linebacker. He would probably give Carl a run for his money. Thomas was all packed energy in a wiry soccer body. This expanse of warm flesh was a tantalizing experience.

I curbed such thoughts when I looked at Piper. She was shooting daggers at me. I was no poker player. Very bad at hiding my emotions. I smiled at her weakly as I slid in the backseat and she retaliated by slamming the door a little harder than necessary.

Piper quickly slipped into the car. I couldn't help but wonder how many words were exchanged before she got in. We couldn't possibly see this guy again, surely Piper knew that?

Once we exited the garage I ventured the topic.

"You know Piper, about this Hunter guy—"

"Don't. Stop right there," she cut me off.

I sighed deeply. "You know you can't see him—"

She cranked up the CD player to drown out my voice and I leaned back in the seat to stew. She could be such a brat sometimes.

By the time we reached Psi Phi House, my knee had knitted itself together nicely. One perk about being a vampire was that we heal quickly. Even half-bloods.

"How's the knee feeling?" Piper inquired from the front seat as though nothing happened.

"Is that the way we're going to play it?" I asked. It was obvious she wasn't taking any advice or orders on this one.

"How's the knee feeling?" she parroted back, so I dropped the subject for now. Of course I knew the issue was far from resolved, but no one was as stubborn as Piper.

"Better. Man, I can't believe I shattered my kneecap. I'm so stupid. Drop and roll, drop and roll," I muttered to myself as I pushed open the door. Piper rushed around to help me out.

"It's not like you meant to," she reminded me sarcastically. I leaned heavily against her, hobbling up to the house.

She opened the back door and helped me inside. Sorority houses, as a rule, were brimming with activity. That many women in close proximity, all with classes, studying and extracurricular activities would keep any house jumping. We see all our action at night. Girls waking up and getting ready to start their day, so to speak.

Many of us can be up and out during the day, if we take precaution with a level billion SPF sunscreen; but then again, some of us can't. You can never tell with a half-blood. Those of us who are so many generations removed from the original vampires can possess many or just a few vampire traits. Full-bloods consider us undesirable. Until last year, we would not have been permitted to exist. That is, until *I* became a half-blood.

"I have to use the little girls' room, can you make it to the living room without me?" Piper asked, doing a little antsy dance.

"Yeah," I assured her as she zipped past me. I noticed Angie in the library as I made my way toward the couches.

"Hurry up!" Angie, one of our original girls, shouted from the library down the hidden staircase to the dormitory. "Nordstrom is gonna close soon and I won't be able to get my stuff."

She looked up and caught my eye, complaining, "I get

that Lizzie can't go in the sun, but why does it still take her a good hour after sundown to get ready?"

I shrugged as I hobbled beyond the library but I could still hear Angie say, "Did you get attacked and hurt your knee again? Drop and roll, Colby."

"Drop and roll, Colby," I muttered to myself, mimicking Angie's well-intended advice. "Yeah, like I didn't think after I was punched— You should try to drop and roll when someone is swinging a sword at you and generally trying to pound you into the ground."

I continued to mutter to myself as I entered the living room and plopped down on one of the oversize couches. I arranged a pillow under my knee and leaned back against the armrest with a sigh.

"I heard you forgot to drop and roll." My aunt came up behind me and peered over the back of the couch.

"Piper?" I asked wearily.

"No, Angie. Piper seemed to be in a mood. Did you two have a fight?"

I watched her as she examined my knee; then, with a satisfied *hmmph*, she sat down on the coffee table next to me instead of choosing one of the fluffy chairs. Aunt Chloe hated fluffy furniture.

"A difference in taste, or maybe not," I said mysteriously.

My aunt chuckled appreciatively. "If I didn't know better, I'd say a boy was involved."

I gaped at her in surprise. "How could you *know* that?"

"Really, Colby, what else is there for two young women to argue about? It's not like you borrow each other's clothes or something."

"It's not like that. See, we were cornered in the shopping center parking garage and some vamps attacked us. Except they were different than regular vampires. They were sort of falling apart and smelled horrendous."

I wrinkled my nose at the memory of the sour-milk odor. "They were out to eliminate us and when I staked them, they dissolved into this toxic goo. I was on my last guy when I slipped on his buddy and went down hard. Piper saved the day and staked him."

Aunt Chloe's eyebrows shot up in surprise.

"Yeah, *I know*. Anyway, when the fight was all over, some big, hunky biker dude showed up to help me off the ground." I paused a moment for dramatic effect.

"What happened then?" Aunt Chloe insisted.

I answered triumphantly:

"Piper threw up on his boots." I smiled at the memory. That should impress the guy.

"Shame on you, Colby Blanchard," she scolded. "You know how hard that must have been for poor Piper. Now about this boy—did he see the fight?"

I shook my head. "No. At least I'm pretty sure he didn't. I mean, if you saw a vampire brawl in a secluded garage, I doubt you would hang around to help the winner. No matter how strong you were."

"So he was strong?" Aunt Chloe said shrewdly.

I squirmed a bit. "Yeah, pretty strong. He carried me to the backseat of Piper's car."

"Sounds like he was a very nice biker dude," she commented.

"Well, okay, I'll give you that but I think he was following me all day. I mean, everywhere I looked, he seemed to be there."

"You don't see many biker dudes hanging out at Westlake Center. At least, not in the stores," she conceded.

"Well, he might not be a biker dude, per se. He's just really tall and broad, like a linebacker. Long, dark hair, about shoulder length. He wore a black duster and biker boots." I remembered the feel of his chest when he held me. "Very solidly built."

"I see," Aunt Chloe murmured, a twinkle in her eye.

"No, you don't see anything," I said, correctly interpreting the look. "He's trouble, Aunt Chloe, I mean it."

"Vampire?" she asked seriously.

"No, just a guy. Smelled like oatmeal raisin cookies, but I'm sure he's trouble."

"Of course he is, dear. Just seems like he might be the kind of trouble Piper wouldn't mind getting into?" she suggested as she stood up. "And maybe her best friend should be a little more supportive."

"Over some guy she'll never see again? They didn't exchange digits or anything. They don't even know each other's last name. Why do I always have to take the high road and apologize?" I struggled to sit upright and watch my aunt walk toward the kitchen.

"Why, because you're the Protector, my dear. And you're usually wrong," she added before disappearing from my sight.

I threw myself back down against the sofa and folded my arms petulantly across my chest.

"I am *not* usually wrong," I muttered to myself, stewing in resentment. I took a moment to rethink the evening and realized we would probably never see the mysterious Hunter again so it wouldn't kill me to let Piper believe she had a shot. The guy had gallantly helped us out and hadn't done anything remotely improper.

"Oh, crap," I said to no one in particular.

"Talking to yourself again?" Piper surprised me by rounding the couch and plopping down on the fluffy chair.

"Always." I smiled at her.

"What? No one will listen to you?" She smirked at me, halfway between being serious and joking.

I winced. "Okay, maybe he's just a nice guy playing Good Samaritan. But he's not all that he seems."

"What do you mean? Just because he happened to be in the garage right after the attack, automatically he is an evil bloodsucker?"

"Well, no, he's not a vampire. But he *was* following me all day when I was shopping. Even bought a pair of glasses from the Sunglass Hut when I stared at him."

Piper raised her eyebrows in question. "He bought a pair of sunglasses and that makes him trouble?"

"No, of course not. What makes him trouble is that he was everywhere I was. In the same stores."

"Downtown has exactly two main department stores next to a small mall. You're bound to see the same people shopping in such close quarters," she reasoned.

"But why shop where I was shopping? Why not spread out a little and go down one of the streets? There are tons of little shops up and down that area."

"Why didn't you?" she countered craftily.

"Because I was meeting you and everything I wanted to look at was right there." She shot me a knowing look and I fortified my position. "That doesn't mean he wasn't following me!"

"Sure, Colby, the hot guy was following you. He couldn't possibly have his own shopping to do. It was all about you."

"Hey, that's not fair!"

Piper stood up and towered over me, her dark eyes flashing. "No, it's not fair, Colby. Not to Hunter and certainly not to me. It isn't always about you, ya know. Not everything in the world revolves around this stupid Prophesy and vampire half-bloods and the whole Undead thing. Sometimes it's just about a nice guy being in the wrong place at the right time."

I looked at her incredulously. "Surely you're not that naïve."

Piper threw up her hands and marched out of the house, throwing open the front door with gusto, practically stomping over Thomas in her rage to leave.

Thomas stepped into the House and looked at me in surprise. "Trouble in paradise?" he guessed.

"Nothing I can't handle. I think. We were attacked by some vampires tonight."

"You okay?" he asked, without his usual tirade about being more careful.

"Yeah, I slipped and broke my kneecap but I think it's healed now." I stood up and put some weight on it experimentally. There was a dull ache, but it held so I was almost good as new.

He plopped himself down in the seat Piper had just vacated and leaned his head back, closing his eyes. "You forgot to drop and roll again?"

I glared at him. Thomas, at least the Thomas *I knew*, would normally have been all over me for details about the vampires. How many? Where did they attack? What did they want? Et cetera. This guy practically falling asleep in a fluffy chair (chairs he hated, BTW) was someone I barely recognized.

First of all, he wasn't driving me crazy with undue concern. Secondly, he looked terrible. My man was beautiful to look at. This guy was a mess. His clothes were rumpled like he'd slept in them, his hair was sticking up all over and he had dark circles under his usually clear green eyes. He obviously wasn't sleeping well. Still.

"I took out four vampires tonight and even Piper got a piece of the action. She saved me from the last one."

"Good to hear," he mumbled.

My gaze narrowed. I hate being ignored. "Then this wicked-looking wizard summoned a fire-breathing dragon and it totally toasted the cars in the parking garage. I subdued it using my hypnotic gaze and chained it outside in the backyard. I'm keeping it for a pet. I'm calling it Snort."

His lips twitched upward. "Snort is a fine name for a dragon."

I threw my hands up in defeat. "What's up with you?"

"I'm just tired, honey. That's all. You remember Carl leaves for New York tomorrow, right? They have bands of rogue vampires roaming the streets at night. They need all the help they can get." He shook his head.

I made a sympathetic clucking sound. I so didn't care if New York City had some vampire issues. They were getting Carl, Thomas's best friend and partner, but they weren't getting Thomas because I needed him more.

I debated telling him the details about our encounter but he looked so tired I decided against it. There would be time later.

"Anything I can do to help?" I moved toward him and sat down on the chair's armrest, running my fingers through his disheveled hair.

"Mmmm. That feels good. You could clear up this whole Prophesy nonsense?" he suggested unnecessarily. He knew it was my major focus morning and night. He wasn't the only one tired of all the chaos. My house was growing by leaps and bounds with unlicensed half-bloods being created by rogues.

"Consider it done," I assured him, massaging his temples.

"Excellent. Now that that's settled . . ." He pulled me down across his lap and kissed me soundly. "So tell me about this vampire attack," he murmured against my neck, trailing kisses everywhere he could reach.

I sighed blissfully until he nipped me, drawing blood. "Hey, you're not horny, you're just hungry!" I accused him, struggling to sit up. He was going for double duty.

"Can't I be both?" he asked, all innocent.

"When did dinner and romance become the same thing, anyway?" I pouted.

He continued to nuzzle my neck and murmured, "When you emancipated half-blood vampires and were ordained by an ancient Prophesy to be the one who would bring about the end of the world as we know it. It kind of upped my workload."

I pulled away and glared at him. "So this is my fault?"

Thomas looked confused. "When did this discussion become about fault? Or blaming anyone? I just wanted to spend some quality time with my girlfriend, doing what vampire couples do. Vampires feed, Colby."

"Yes, I know vampires feed, Thomas. I do it myself on occasion." I squirmed out of his lap, annoyed he was blaming me for his busy schedule and double-duty antics.

"How did this turn into a fight?" he asked, mystified by my anger. He was such a guy.

"We're not fighting, we're talking about my most recent attack," I assured him woodenly.

He ground his teeth in frustration. "Fine, tell me about this attack."

"No. I don't want to now."

Thomas groaned, rubbing his eyes as though to clear his head. "You're impossible. You know that?"

"Funny, I thought I was a Happy Meal." I stood over him, hands on hips.

"I'm going back to bed. This is obviously a bad dream." Thomas pulled himself wearily out of the chair and headed toward the upstairs rooms.

"Just where do you think you're going?" I demanded.

"To find another Happy Meal," he retorted sarcastically.

"Oh, ha-ha," I muttered once he left the room.

Why did he make me so crazy? The poor guy was just tired! Did I really have to make such a big deal over the love nip? The truth of the matter was Thomas hadn't been acting like himself for the last month. He was always tired, never seeming to relax. He was so busy at work, I couldn't begin to guess why he agreed to let New York borrow Carl. We had rogue vampire activity here, so why send one of our best Vampire Investigators away? I had tried to talk him out of it but he insisted it was the right thing to do.

Instead of following Thomas upstairs to apologize, I went downstairs to see what was going on. Most of the girls were watching television in the rec room when I plopped down on the carpet and leaned against the ottoman.

I sneezed violently. Once. Then again. "Okay, who snuck a cat in here?" I demanded.

Sophie looked guilty at once. Next to me, she had the world's worse poker face. She was Ileana's human maid and she loved stray animals.

"Soph-ie. You know I'm allergic. No cats in Psi Phi House. That's a rule. Now where is it?" I felt like the Grinch when she scurried over to the sleeping dorm and opened the door. Sure enough, a scraggly calico emerged, meowing a pitiful hello.

It was one ugly cat. Which could mean only one thing. It belonged to Mrs. Murphy. Every neighborhood had one of those cat ladies and ours was no exception. About a block over was a lady who was a hundred and three if she was a day, and her house was filled with cats. And they were never cute. They all seemed to suffer from mange.

"You need to take it back to Mrs. Murphy," I said, ignoring the look on Sophie's face. She picked up the cat and it was hard to say who looked more forlorn, the calico or Sophie.

"I can't take it back. That crazy ol' lady accused me of stealing her cats. Said she was going to call the police on me next time."

Sophie came straight from Ileana's English estate and possessed the sweetest British accent. She was tough to refuse.

"She wouldn't think you were stealing her cats if you stopped feeding the strays that wander away from there. That's why she thinks you're a catnapper."

Sophie hung her head in shame, cuddling the filthy cat, which purred in response.

"So not gonna work on me," I declared firmly. I wasn't falling for the poor English waif and her widdle, biddy kitty act. She let out a big sigh and held out the cat to me.

"Dude, I'm not gonna take it. I *can't*. Allergies, remember?" As though to prove a point, I let out a huge sneeze. You would think being Undead would cure me of allergies but no; if anything, it made them worse.

Sage chose just that moment to step into the basement living room. She took one look at the scene before her and tried to sneak back up the stairs.

"Sage, perfect timing," I called to her in a falsetto voice.

"You want me to take Fluffy back to Mrs. Murphy's house?" she accurately guessed.

"You know its name?" I asked, surprised.

"She calls all her cats Fluffy."

Of course, in a weird way, that made total sense. She was

blind as a bat and it would be much easier to call them for dinner if they had the same name.

"If you wouldn't mind . . ."

"Yeah okay." She approached Sophie and took her kitty burden. "Phew, this cat needs a bath." Sage wrinkled her nose.

The cat, as if understanding Sage's statement, started to squirm in her arms.

"Relax, Fluffy, you're safe with me. I'm just the delivery girl, not the cat laundress." They trudged upstairs.

I turned to Sophie. "Really, no more cats. I know it's hard for you being so far from home and all, but I just can't do cats."

"What about a different pet? Just a little one," she rushed to reassure me. "I'd take care of it and it wouldn't be any trouble at all. I promise."

I gave in. "If you keep it in your room and Ileana agrees, then it's fine by me. But you'll be in charge of taking care of it and stuff."

"Oh, thank you, miss." Sophie gave me a spontaneous hug and bounded up the stairs. Presumably to garner Ileana's support. At least I wouldn't have to worry about any more cats in the house. There was certainly an upside to such a decision.

Four

PIPER

'd promised Carl I would see him before he took off so I headed in that direction when I left Psi Phi House. But I was in a mood. I spent my free time going to self-defense class and researching Undead issues all because my best friend was a self-centered cheerleader turned vampire and the only thing that changed about her during the attack was her breathing status. She was so full of herself sometimes, it drove me nuts. I tried to shake off the mood when I got to Carl's apartment.

"I have something for you," he said to me after I arrived. I raised an eyebrow in surprise. "Like I haven't heard that one before."

I swear, he almost blushed. It was fun teasing Carl. He was Thomas's best friend and a dedicated Vampire Investigator. He could be so serious at times, but he also had a very dry sense of humor. He was a mixed bag.

"Ha, very funny. What I have for you is a window of opportunity. And get your mind out of the gutter, it's not *that* kind of opportunity. You Breathers are all alike. Just one thing on your minds."

"You big tease." I pouted. "And don't call me a Breather. You know how I hate that," I added, only slightly serious. Yeah, I hated the term "Breather" since it was considered an insult by the vampire community, but Carl always used it as more of an endearment.

He ignored me and continued, "I have for you a gift of such magnitude, you will be forever in my debt." He rubbed his hands together like a villain in the old movies.

"You're loaning me your apartment while you're in New York?" I perked up at the idea of using his bachelor pad as my own while he was doing a transfer assignment on the East Coast.

"I said I had a gift, not that I was delusional," he replied dryly, effectively dampening my enthusiasm.

I plopped down on the bar stool. "Oh, fine. What is it, then?"

He walked around the bar and pulled a manila envelope out of the drawer. He slid it across the counter toward me.

"Giving me my walking papers? Did you have them notarized?"

"Just open it, smart-ass."

I tore the envelope open with my short thumbnail, quickly

checking the black polish for chips before dumping the envelope's contents onto the counter.

A key, a swipe card and a folded piece of paper.

"Gee, however will I be able to repay you?" I said woodenly, not understanding his gift.

He picked up the key. "This opens the basement door to the vampire archives." He showed me the slide card. "This opens the front door after hours and this"—he waved the paper in my direction—"is the Tribunal Security schedule for a special delivery."

I looked at him blankly.

He sighed in exasperation. "If you look at the schedule, you will notice that the library will be unoccupied for two hours. No one, living or otherwise, will be in the library during that time. There is a new display I think you will find very interesting." He looked at me meaningfully.

"Oh!" I sat up straighter, finally catching his meaning. Carl was giving me access to the ancient scripts in the library without Colby or any other vampire knowing about it.

I grabbed the paper from him and looked over the schedule carefully. "Won't you get in trouble for this?"

"Only if you're caught. You can manage to do this without getting caught, can't you?" He made a threatening gesture to grab the paper out of my hand.

"Of course I can do this without getting caught. Sheesh, what poor faith you have in my abilities." My stomach knotted up at the thought of breaking into a vampire library.

Colby was the brave one. I was sort of the sarcastic sidekick. Heavy on wit, light on actual daring.

My face must have relayed my fears because he seemed to waver. "Piper, you don't have to do this. I know you want to help Colby with this whole Prophesy thing but there is no need for you to, uh, take any unnecessary risks."

I threw him a disgusted look. "I won't be taking any risks if your schedule is right. It *is* right, isn't it?"

It was his turn to look disgusted. "Of course it's right. You don't think I would put you in danger, do you?"

"I don't know." I pretended to contemplate his question. "I mean, you *could* get rid of a Breather . . ."

He laughed at me. "True, there is that. But then I'm leaving anyway, so I get rid of you either way, don't I?"

I instantly sobered. "So you're leaving soon then?"

"Yep, tomorrow."

"Do you really have to go? You're needed here." It was the closest thing to a confession I was going to make. Carl was, well, Carl. Tall, dark, handsome and Undead. Not boyfriend material but he was a great Vampire Investigator, and after our run-in with those stinky vampires, I didn't want one of the best headed to New York City.

"Surely they have Investigators there." I didn't like the way my voice took on a whiny quality, almost like I was pleading.

Carl walked around the bar and took both my hands in his. As always, I was surprised by how cool he was to touch.

I used to wonder if things would be different between us if we were both living. Not that it mattered. He was Undead and I wasn't and things weren't going to change. Still, I cared about Carl and wanted him to be happy. Ever since Thomas found Colby, there was a restlessness in Carl. Much like the restlessness that invaded me at odd moments. A sort of discontent that I just wasn't willing to analyze further. I didn't need someone to make me complete. Did I?

Still, having someone to go out with, to call and be with didn't sound like such a bad deal either. Like what Colby and Thomas had. I couldn't believe I was envying Colby. I mean, even dead the girl managed to still have it all.

"You and Psi Phi House are going to be fine, Piper. New York needs help. I wouldn't be going if it weren't an emergency. Rogue vampire activity is at an all-time high. There's something in the air," he added cryptically.

"Yeah, I know and a lot of it's still here in Seattle." I tugged my hands out of his and jumped off the bar stool. "It's like you don't even care."

"I don't care? You think I'm leaving because I don't care?" His mood changed abruptly and he threw up his hands in frustration. "Between you and Thomas I can't seem to win."

"What does that mean?"

"It means that I'm a Vampire Investigator. It's not just a job, it's who I am. I swore an oath to protect all vampires and that includes half-bloods now, as well. New York has a desperate need for Investigators. I have to go. It's my job. Thomas understands that. Sure, I had reservations about leaving but he made me see the light. He can handle things here. I have to go where I am needed. And right now, that's NYC."

"Wait a minute. *Thomas* wants you to go?" I couldn't believe what I was hearing. Did Thomas really think everything was so safe and secure here that he was going to send one of his best Vampire Investigators away?

"He said they needed me and that's why I'm going. I trust his judgment, Piper. You should too. Anyway, Thomas will be here and he has the entire Tribunal Security at his beck and call. Colby can take care of herself, and she's got your back too."

I nodded, but doubt filled me. Why would Thomas send Carl away? Didn't he think these attacks were something to be concerned about? Colby said Thomas wasn't getting enough sleep and was plagued by bad dreams—maybe it was affecting his judgment? No, I was being ridiculous. I just didn't want Carl to go away. He was one of the few people who "got" me.

I stepped toward Carl and wrapped my arms around his torso. At first he stood still; then slowly, he awkwardly put his arms around me, as if afraid I would break with the least amount of pressure, and we stood embracing in the middle of his apartment. He smelled wonderful, clean and rugged at the same time.

Carl was dear to me, though we could never be more than friends. He held a special place in my heart.

"You be safe," I whispered into his chest.

He stroked my hair and I felt his lips brush the top of my head. "Everything's going to be fine. You'll see."

"I hope you're right," I murmured. I was afraid things were going to get worse. Much worse.

Five

COLBY

Entering the offices of the Vampire Tribunal was much like entering any law office in downtown Seattle. They enjoyed sprawling views of the Sound, were located on the upper levels of the Columbia Tower and felt stuffy and respectable. No one would suspect that they housed the most powerful vampire leaders in the Clan.

Margaret Durham was seated at the reception desk, like always. Neatly put together in a St. John knit pantsuit, hair swept up and tidily clipped to her head, she gave the impression of prestigious gatekeeper to the influential men seated behind the doors. And she hated me. A lot.

"Hello, Margaret," I greeted her.

She didn't even bother to look up from her computer monitor. "Go away, he's busy."

This was our relationship in a nutshell.

"Come on, Margaret. He actually *asked* to see me. I'm

not just dropping by unannounced." Which was kind of the truth. Mr. Holloway said I could come by anytime I had a problem. And today, well, I had a problem.

"He's in a meeting," she replied, not even pretending to check his schedule.

I made a loud groaning noise as I advanced to the glass fortress she called a desk.

"Please," I whined.

"No," she said, but her lips held a ghost of a smile. She loved it when I begged. She was a full-blood vampire bigot and I was trying to be nice. It was killing me.

"Fine, I'll just hang out here with you and catch up on all the Undead gossip."

She continued to type away at her computer, ignoring me. Yeah, like I could be ignored for long.

"No news? Okay, well I have a ton of stuff to share. Did you know PSU has a sorcery degree program? Yeah, I know. I had no idea either. So the girls are calling PSU Para-Super U. Get it? Instead of Puget Sound University they are nicknaming it Paranormal Supernatural University and shortening the name to Para-Super U. How funny is that? Oh, and that Sophie keeps collecting cats and as you know, I'm terribly allergic to—"

She slammed her hands on her keyboard.

"Fine, you win. Go see him. Just leave me alone." She buzzed to let me through.

"Thanks, Margaret!" I maneuvered through the reception hall to Mr. Holloway's door. I was an expert on not being ignored. Ask my mom. Whenever she was busy with house listings and I needed something, she'd learned to stop what she was doing and help me. I could be that annoying. Call it a gift.

I rapped on the heavy mahogany door, and then turned the knob.

"Mr. Holloway?"

He was seated at a large, impressive desk, going through paperwork. I kind of felt sorry for vampires now. Once they were primal beings, feeding and battling for supremacy, and now they were a bunch of bureaucrats, sifting through red tape and making laws to ensure their existence. It was no secret that the older a vampire got, the crazier they were likely to become. They got paranoid, reclusive and untrusting. Only the vampires with lifelong companions, friends or lovers seemed to keep it together.

"Colby, my dear. What brings you to me?"

That was a favorable start. He was usually so busy with vampire business I rarely got more than a moment of his time.

"I was hoping you had a minute. I have some interesting news that I'd like your take on."

"I hope it's more pressing than the renaming of PSU to Para-Super U or your cat allergies." He offered me a chair.

"How did you . . . ?"

"Vampire hearing, Colby." He tapped his ear.

"Ah, well, sorry about that." I was a bit embarrassed being caught acting like such an obnoxious brat by the boss man.

"I believe you two have a bit of a blind spot about each other."

"Why, Mr. Holloway," I declared, doing my best Scarlett O'Hara impression. "Whatever do you mean?" I fanned myself lightly.

He chuckled. "My dear, you are amusing. I'll give you that. Now what news have you brought me?"

I settled into the chair he offered and debated the best way to begin.

"I had an unusual encounter this evening. Not my typical kind," I rushed to assure him before he could tell me to take it up with Thomas and dismiss me. "But with a different type of vampire."

"Go on."

"Well, you see, these vampires were kind of squishy. Sort of decaying. In fact, if I had to call it something, I would say they were zombie vampires."

I peeked up at him through my lashes, ready to be thrown out of his office for wasting his time.

"I see," he said, leaning back in his chair and crossing his arms over his torso. My eyes were immediately drawn to his right hand, where he wore his vampire license. I could see the scar under his ring at the base of his finger where he'd cut it off so many years ago and then put it back to knit together.

Shaking my head, I continued with my story. "They also smelled bad. I mean really bad. Like rotten eggs, expired dairy bad. And when they were staked, a white mist escaped into the air."

"How many have you encountered so far, Colby?" He didn't seem the least bit surprised by my description. I wasn't sure if that was a good sign or not.

"There were five total, all dead now. And I mean really dead, not like Undead," I felt the need to clarify, then coughed to clear my throat.

"I understand the distinction."

"I was kind of hoping you could shed some light on what these guys were."

Please don't say zombies, please don't say zombies, I chanted in my head.

"They are demon-possessed vampires. Zombies, by a more common name."

Crap, I asked you not to call them that.

"Do they want to eat my brains?" I had to know.

"I wouldn't think so. Zombies have no need of sustenance, so have no desire to consume anything. They are merely a vessel being used by the demon possessing them. They have no agenda of their own."

Well, there's another great horror-movie myth shot down by cold, hard fact. I mean, I was glad there weren't zombies roaming the earth eating brains but at the same time, I wanted to believe pop culture got some things right once in a while.

"I don't understand. Why would demons want to possess a vampire if they didn't want to eat my brains? I have rogue vampires trying to kick my butt on a regular basis—why do demons want in on the action?"

"The Prophesy, of course."

"I thought you didn't take stock in the Prophesy. You said it was a bunch of superstitious nonsense."

He stood up and walked around the room. "Colby, it doesn't matter if I believe the Prophesy. It doesn't matter if you believe it either. What matters is that *they* believe it." He swept his arm out toward the window, with its breathtaking view of the city.

"If enough vampires believe the Prophesy is real, it becomes self-fulfilling. Do you understand?"

I hated to say this. "Uh, no."

"What I mean is that if you believe the end of your existence is inevitable, you will take certain actions. You might take risks or join with forces you would not normally contemplate in a bid to survive. These actions become the catalyst. Those that believe in the Prophesy actually become the ones who make it happen."

"And you think vampires are joining forces with these demons in a bid to survive?" I was still totally confused.

"No, demons don't work that way. Demons are opportunists. They need to be in the right place at the right time. They can only possess a body with no soul. And the demon must be present when the soul leaves the body. It's all very carefully timed. Secondly, most demons are content to stay in their own plane of existence."

"Why?"

"It's their home, of course. It's where they live, play and exist. But occasionally, a demon comes along who wants more. Who dreams of conquering others. He rallies his fellow demons and uses something like the Prophesy as an opportunity to further his cause. These demons are rare. That's why you don't see a lot of demon possessions."

"But you think that such a demon might be making a play now?" I was catching on.

"Yes. Tell me, Colby, what do you know about demons?"

"Oh well, I know they—that is to say they, honestly, I don't know anything, sir."

He walked to his whiteboard and picked up a marker. "There are seven kinds of demons, Colby. Some are of no consequence; they are harmless or uninterested in possession. The one we need to be concerned with is an Avarice Demon named Barnaby."

I looked at the names he wrote on the board. Seven in total. "Avarice Demon? You mean greed? This demon is greedy?"

"Not exactly. This demon *is* greed. Do you get the distinction?"

I really wanted to be head pupil on this one but I still needed a little more help. I shook my head.

Mr. Holloway sighed. "It's not your fault, Colby. You're young and only in your first year, right? It's no matter. Barnaby, that's the name of this particular Avarice Demon, wants to take over our world. To do that he needs to get as many demons to follow him as possible. They can't possible infiltrate enough humans in a short period of time without an epidemic or a war. Those are difficult to predict and frankly, humans are too fragile. Barnaby is not a patient demon. Instead, he will use vampires."

"But how do you possess something that is Undead?"

"By replacing the missing part of a vampire's essence with themselves. They can only enter slowly, through dreams and unguarded moments. The vampire suspects something is going on, but demons are smart. They tend to choose vampires that isolate themselves from others and then drive that vampire crazy with paranoid delusions and irrational thoughts. Haven't you wondered why there is so much rogue activity lately?"

I jumped out of my chair. "You mean all those vampires going rogue are really becoming possessed by demons? How do we stop it?"

"By stopping the leader, my dear. By stopping Barnaby."

"Tell me where to find him." I had no idea how to fight a demon but I was mad enough to wing it.

"You can't kill a demon in his own dimension, Colby. You can't reach him, nor could you survive there. He must cross over. It is only when the demon is fully ingrained that it can be annihilated. The biggest challenge is not destroying the vampire to kill the demon. Physical signs alert us when a

vampire has been fully possessed: completely irrational behavior, putrid, decaying flesh. By then it's too late."

"So demons possess the Undead and they, in turn, attack
other Undead. We are killing ourselves, making the Prophesy
come true. And I get the blame."

"I'm sorry, my dear, but I believe that is what's happening."

"But I've got to stop it!" I certainly wasn't a huge fan of
vampires in general but I didn't want the entire species wiped
out because some greedy demon wanted a new plane of existence to hang out in.

"I fear the only way to stop it is to destroy Barnaby—but
no one knows where he will strike next."

There had to be a way. If Barnaby was using the Prophesy
to achieve his endgame, then I needed to use it to beat him.

"I need access to the vampire library and everything in it.
Restricted or otherwise."

"You have a plan?" He seemed surprised by my rally.

"Beat the bad guy, save the world."

He looked at me.

"Well, it's more of a mantra than a plan. But I do think I
can figure out Baranaby's next move with a little research.
Know thy enemy and all that stuff."

He nodded in agreement and picked up the phone. I now
had full access to the library.

"What else do you need?" It was go time.

Six

PIPER

"It could be Elven. I have a friend who speaks Elven. Maybe he can take a look at it?"

I blew air out of my mouth in frustration. "You know, Wayne, if it isn't Klingon, I'm going out on a limb and sayin' it probably isn't Elvish either. Thanks anyway."

I was officially at a dead end. Wayne was the last of a long list of dead ends. It wasn't Persian, Latin, Chinese, Egyptian or, thank goodness, Klingon. The Prophesy's original text was a complete and utter friggin' mystery. Still.

"Looks like ancient Runic," a deep voice whispered in my ear, tickling my neck and sending my pulse racing.

"You!" I exclaimed, rather uncoolly. "I mean, hey, Hunter. What a surprise."

Wayne took one look at Hunter, with his tall, muscular body and windblown, shoulder-length hair, and practically raced out of the teahouse.

Hunter smirked at Wayne's hasty departure while making himself comfortable in his still-warm seat. I raised an eyebrow at his forwardness. God, I loved a man with confidence.

"Would you jump in my grave as quick?" It was something my grandpa always said to us kids when we scrambled to take possession of his favorite recliner after he got up to use the bathroom. I was never sure quite what it meant but it seemed appropriate for the moment.

"Do you always start conversations with grave references?" Hunter asked smoothly.

"Do you really know anything about Runic language?" I challenged back, trying to play it as cool as he was acting. I frowned at the paper in front of me.

He shrugged indifferently. Oh boy, he was so hot.

"Prove it to me." I pushed the page in his direction.

He leaned forward, pointing to the symbols on the page. "See how the letters are all at an angle? Like slash marks? Runic is ancient. Back when important messages were carved on wood or stone. See here, it's easier to carve a straight slash than a curve." He slid a switchblade from his boot and demonstrated by slashing the air in lines.

I think he was trying to shock me by pulling out a blade to make his point, but I'd seen Undead implode. A little ol' knife was not going to freak me out.

I ignored him and analyzed the letters again. "Huh," I grunted. He might have something there. "Now how come five other college students and one professor had no idea what this language was?"

"Probably because it isn't straight Runic. It looks like a mixture of Runic with something else. Perhaps Ogden script? See, these letters are different. Also, Ogden script is read from left to right while these here are read from right to left."

"Ogden script?" I was completely baffled.

Hunter tucked his knife neatly back into his boot. "Ogden script is another ancient language. Used by tree priests."

I stared at him in wonder and disbelief. Who was this guy that he had a working knowledge of ancient scripts about trees, anyway?

"So what does that mean?" I asked, completely confused.

"It means someone combined two very different ancient languages and married them in some way. To create a language or code only they could understand."

"But you understand it?" I ventured, curious.

He leaned back and smiled. "Maybe. What's it for?"

I debated on what to tell him. After all, I didn't know this guy at all, but I really wouldn't mind the prospect of a little one-on-one tutoring from him. However, the last time I met him he happened to arrive on the scene of a very messy vampire tussle where Colby was hurt and almost staked. She was convinced he was trouble, so I couldn't really spill the beans about vampires and ancient prophesies. Not to mention it would make me sound crazy.

"Scavenger hunt. Part of Greek Week."

He raised an eyebrow at me in question. "You don't strike me as a Greek."

"I'm not. Just helping out a friend. She wants to win really bad."

He looked unconvinced. I smiled benignly.

"Your friend from the other day, Colby, is it?"

"Yeah, that's her. She's very competitive." It annoyed me he remembered her name, though I couldn't say why. Everyone remembered Colby. Blonde hair, perfect figure. She was larger than life. And by assuming it was Colby, he was basically saying I had no other friends, wasn't he?

"She okay?" he asked, apparently buying my scavenger hunt story. That annoyed me too. Did I look like the kind of gal who would waste her time on a Greek Week activity? Hello? Not so much.

I stamped down my annoyance. "Colby? Oh yeah. She's fine."

"She's so little," he commented.

"She's small, but she's wiry," I assured him sharply. Did we have to go on about Colby's tiny, frail figure?

"Good to know." Sometimes, it was tough having a friend like Colby. Little Miss Sunshine girl. Even now that she was a half-blood vampire she still lit up a room. She could at least have become a stereotypical vampire and gone all dark and morbid but no, Colby had to do things her own way. Like always.

"What's with the sigh?" Hunter asked.

I shook my head. "This scavenger hunt is becoming a huge pain in my rear. Do you really think you might be able to decipher this message?"

He picked up the paper, reviewed it closely and looked back at me. He seemed to be contemplating his answer, measuring his words carefully before saying them aloud.

"I might be able to but I don't have enough to go by. Do you have more of this writing?"

My heart sank. No, I didn't have more ancient texts. In fact, any texts were going to be at the vampire library and who knew if I could make copies of the stuff there? If it wasn't on display, I wouldn't even know what to look for. One script looked very much like another to me and Hunter had taken all of three seconds to figure out it was actually two ancient alphabets used together.

I had a crazy, wild, irrational thought. No, I couldn't. Colby would kill me. Of course, she didn't know Carl gave me access to the library and she'd forbidden me from going anyway because of the danger factor. What if Hunter were to accompany me? He could act as my bodyguard, and he certainly didn't need to know we were breaking into a vampire library, did he?

"Why are you here, anyway?" I asked bluntly.

"Tea is the new coffee, haven't you heard?"

"But you're not drinking any tea."

He refused to break eye contact. "No, it doesn't appear that I am, does it?"

"How did you find me?"

"What makes you think I was looking for you?" Haughty was so sexy. I needed professional help, didn't I?

"And yet, here you are."

"Coincidence?" he ventured.

"Unlikely."

"Maybe someone told me I would find you here."

"Who?" I asked sharply.

"Someone at Psi Phi House."

My heart raced. How did he know about Psi Phi House? Who was he anyway?

"Your car had a Psi Phi House sticker in the window so I did a little checking. Only one sorority called Psi Phi and it happens to be at PSU. Very convenient, since I live on Capital Hill."

"So you were looking for me."

"Maybe I was looking for your little blonde friend?" he countered.

"She's not here. I am," I said. Why was I surprised? Of course he was interested in Colby.

"Lucky me."

I didn't know what to say to that. He was way better at the cool, sophisticated banter than I was. I decided to switch the conversation back to where I was in control.

"How do you know so much about these scripts, anyway?"

He stared at me a moment more before saying, "My grandfather," without elaborating.

"And?" I drawled after a moment.

"And when I was little, I would stay with him in his huge house full of all sorts of books and journals. He loved ancient languages but preferred pagan symbols above all others. He devoted most of his time to their study after he retired."

"Oh, what did he used to do?" What kind of job leads you to spend your free time studying old languages? Was he an archaeologist or something?

"That would be a story for another time," Hunter said confidently, annoying and thrilling me at the same time.

"What makes you think there's going to be another time?" I scoffed. Two could play at this game.

"You need me," he said simply.

Instead of immediately dousing his ego with a white-hot put-down guaranteed to make even the most confident of men cry like a little girl, I studied him.

Somewhere in that gorgeous, brooding noggin was the knowledge I needed to help Colby and the girls of Psi Phi. It was dangerous and probably foolhardy but the high risk was worth it if I solved the riddle. Colby was living on borrowed time and so was the world if that stupid Prophesy was to be believed. I *did* need Hunter. He was kind of my last hope. And it didn't hurt that he was something to look at as well. I needed to be bold.

"Will you come somewhere with me? And not ask any questions and do exactly what I say?"

His look intensified, if that was even possible. "On one condition."

God, there was always a condition, wasn't there? I slowly nodded.

"I get to drive." He pointed out the teahouse window to an illegally parked motorcycle.

*   *   *

We met again at Psi Phi House early Wednesday. If he had reservations about going someplace unknown at five in the morning, he kept it to himself. He was true to his word.

I'd never been on a motorcycle before. It was a thrilling experience. The engine vibrating beneath me while I held on tight to Hunter made my knees weak. I could get used to traveling that way. As long as I was with Hunter. He was in control and confident. He was totally comfortable with who he was and I was drawn to him.

Colby would say it was his bad-boy demeanor that turned me on, but it was more than that. I felt like we were connected somehow. It was weird; I couldn't put my finger on it, but Hunter and I were cut from the same cloth.

It was still about an hour before daybreak; I could tell Hunter was surprised when we stopped at our destination.

"You wanted to take me to a lakeside house without asking any questions? Do you think the house doesn't know it's on the lake or something?" He was being sarcastic of course, but I wasn't sure why. He seemed very disappointed. Did he think I was taking him on a bank heist or something?

I jumped off the back of his bike and returned the borrowed helmet. "Boy, you don't like not knowing what's coming next, do you?"

He unbuttoned his duster, took off his own helmet and replied, "You have no idea."

"Follow me." I walked quietly across the gravel driveway, to the side of the house. The basement door was the entrance directly into the library. Vampires usually entered the house through the front door. At least, that's what Colby mentioned once.

"Piper?"

"Huh?" I kept looking around for signs of anyone moving around in the house.

"Why are you tiptoeing?"

I looked down and sure enough, I was on the toes of my canvas high-tops, trying not to make any noise. "I don't like the sound gravel makes when you step on it."

Mark that down as the lamest excuse, ever.

"Uh-huh." Hunter looked at me like I was crazy. Which I surely was if I was taking him into a vampire library. I pushed that thought aside. We came to the door and I took out the card.

I waved it in front of the pad and the blinking light went from red to green. I pushed the door and it swung open easily. No blaring alarms or sirens announced our entrance. I let out a big sigh of relief.

Hunter gave me a questioning look so I said, "Sometimes the door sticks."

Inside were rows of books, like any other library. I walked down the first aisle slowly, trying to get my bearings. I noted the checkout desk in the back of the room, with two doors behind it. Both were closed, and both had locks on the door-knobs.

"Where to now?" Hunter asked, making me jump.

"I'm not sure. Just keep your eyes open for more of the text I showed you. I think we might find something in the back room. Follow me."

I led him to the back of the library, to the locked doors, and tried my key on one. The door swung open easily. Yay me! Inside were two copy machines, extra paper and office supplies. Clearly I'd found the supply room.

"Oops." We backed out and I went to the other door. I used the key, but this time it didn't turn. I tried again and it still didn't turn. Now what?

"I think you need both the card and the key, like this," Hunter took the card from my pocket and swiped the side of the lock, then tried turning the key and voilà, it opened.

"How'd you know to do that?"

"I'm not just another pretty face, you know,"

"Clearly," I agreed and we entered the second room.

This room had a vault-like quality: several pages of text were framed behind glass that was wired to an alarm system of some kind.

"Over there." I pointed out one particular frame that seemed familiar. Hunter investigated.

"You have that one already," he concluded after looking it over.

"I do? But it looks like this has more text." I pulled out the sheet of paper that held the Prophesy.

"This is an etching, see? This paper was actually put on the stone or wood where the original message was carved and then someone sketched over the paper to pick up the engraving."

"Show me." I peered over his shoulder.

He traced the symbols with his finger and I checked them against the paper in my hand. All the symbols matched. The only difference was the size of the document.

"So these are the exact same? There're no symbols that have been transposed or copied incorrectly?" I gave him the paper to double check.

"No, everything looks the same." He handed it back to me and my heart felt tighter. That just left a translation error. Part of me had hoped someone wrote down the original symbols incorrectly, which would have changed the meaning of the text, but it looked like the symbols were perfectly transcribed. Crap!

"You look like someone just ran over your cat."

"I don't have a cat, I'm a dog person," I replied, not willing to comment on the meaning of his statement.

"Smart girl," he replied but I didn't ask what he meant; I was too bummed about our discovery.

Hunter walked around the room and stopped in front of another frame. He seemed frozen in place so I went to investigate his find.

It was an artful symbol, not like the others I was now familiar with. The sweeping shape wrapped around angular lines was very pretty and yet haunting at the same time. I flipped over my Prophesy page and quickly sketched the symbol.

"What is it, do you think?" I asked Hunter, who didn't respond.

He'd gone very pale and I was worried he'd fall over where he stood. I reached up to steady him when he grabbed my wrist in a painful grasp.

"Is this some sort of joke?" he hissed at me, his color returning.

I looked at the wall and then at him in confusion. "What are you talking about? What does it say?"

He released me suddenly and backed out of the room. I rubbed my wrist, taking one last look at the picture that had so upset him. He obviously knew what it meant and I doubted he was going to share that knowledge with me. What could it possibly say and why would Hunter react so strongly to it?

I left the room, careful to see that it locked behind us. I checked my watch and realized we should probably wrap things up. I found Hunter two aisles down, reading the titles of books on the shelves.

"What kind of place is this?" he asked me, not bothering to turn around when he spoke.

"What do you mean?" I hedged. I couldn't really tell him it was a vampire library but I should have thought the titles of the books here might give it away.

"This book is called *You Can't Go Home Again: Rebuilding After the Change*."

"Uh, clearly this book is about uh, menopause. Right, see. The change is going through menopause. Didn't your mother or grandmother ever talk about the change to you?" I took the volume out of his hands and stuck it back on the shelf, babbling the whole time. "All my grandmother talked about was the change and how she suffered from hot flashes and mood swings. Never knowing when her period was going to arrive . . ."

Hunter was staring at me like I'd gone off the deep end. I shrugged. "It's a real pain in the butt never knowing when you're gonna start your monthly, you know. I can see why women going through the change would be cranky about that."

I'd seen my mother use this tactic on my father many times and it always worked. Bring up feminine things to guys and they couldn't get out of the room fast enough. I was glad to see Hunter was no exception to the rule.

"Are we done here?" he asked.

"Yes, I think we can go now."

"What about the symbols you need?"

"I'm not totally out of options yet. I can check one more place." I reached the door to leave and pushed on it without swiping the card. Simulated sun lights flooded the room, bright like the sun, and an alarm blared. Hunter threw his arm around me, using his duster to cover my head, and shoved us out the door with lightening speed.

We raced to his motorcycle and sprayed gravel in our haste to leave the driveway. Once we were safely on the road and it was obvious no one was chasing us, he slowed down. Both our hearts were racing and I hugged him tighter as he drove. That was a close one. I should be grateful that Hunter reacted so quickly to get us out of there, but I couldn't help wondering if it wasn't the first time he'd jumped on his bike and made a quick escape.

He drove us back to the House as the sun just started to peek over the horizon. He sort of dumped me off on the front lawn and shouted he'd call me, then rode off into the dawn. I guess I couldn't blame him for getting away from me as fast as possible. I did almost get him killed, even if he only thought the biggest risk was getting arrested for breaking and entering.

I went into the House, pleasantly surprised by the quietness around me. Dawn was when good little vampire girls and boys were going to bed. Except half-bloods. They only possessed some vampire traits, so many of them kept the same hours now as they had when they were alive.

I hoped I could catch Ileana before she crawled into her coffin, or whatever she slept in, for the night. I took the stairs two by two. Though most of the girls at Psi Phi slept in the dorms in the secret basement, Ileana preferred to sleep upstairs with her personal human maid, Sophie.

I walked quietly down the hallway, carefully listening for any noise to indicate if someone were sleeping or out and about. I arrived at Ileana's and pressed my ear to the door.

"For goodness' sake, Piper, you walk like an elephant. Come in," Ileana said from inside.

That's what I get for trying to be quiet in a vampire house! Sure, not everyone possessed super vampire hearing but you could bet at least one person did.

"Sorry to wake you," I said as I entered, carefully checking the floor of the entryway for Sophie. The maid usually slept by the door or outside it to guard her charge. Ileana Romanav was a half-blood who'd managed to hide from persecution for more than one hundred years by masquerading as a new family member every generation. She'd pretended to be her great-great-grandmother, great-grandmother, grandmother, and mother, and now she was just Ileana. Thanks to Colby emancipating half-bloods, she was a free Undead. You'd think she would be a little grateful but Ileana was royalty, which might account for the attitude.

"Why are you skulking about the house at this hour?" Ileana asked, sitting pretty in her large canopy bed while Sophie brushed her gorgeous blonde curls.

"Oh, you know me. Skulking is what I do." I looked around the room for the old journals her whacked-out father used to keep. She guessed my intention immediately.

"Sorry, they aren't here. I gave them to Colby, though I don't know what good they'll do her. Or you for that matter."

Ileana didn't believe in the Prophesy. Her father had worshipped vampires, had longed to become one. He served them and did their bidding, and the only thing he got for his devotion was brutally murdered and a half-blood daughter. Ileana had no deep affection for full-bloods or her father, for that matter.

"Why you two persist in researching this Prophesy nonsense is beyond me. I told you I don't believe in the silly thing and yet you two act like the world is coming to an end or something."

"What if it is?" I countered. What made her so sure she was right about the Prophecy being bogus anyway?

"Dear Piper, the world has been around a long time before we came upon it and I daresay it will still be here for a fair amount of time after we leave."

"I don't mean the *literal* world, Ileana, I'm talking about vampires and humans. Our *existence* in this world."

Sophie paused in her brushing and looked at her mistress in question. "Do you really think that Colby is capable of bringing the end of existence as we know it?"

Ileana tried to trivialize my question. "She can't even match her shoes to her outfit. Why, today she had on ballet flats with her jeans! Truly, I don't know how she manages to get to school in one piece sometimes."

Sophie went back to brushing her hair. I looked at Ileana and she smiled back blankly, but her eyes darted toward her maid momentarily. I nodded and changed the subject to something less distressful . . . something Sophie would enjoy.

"So Sophie, smuggle any cats in lately?"

"No, just the one, miss. Colby made me take it back to that crazy lady. She has so many cats, she can't possible take care of all of them. And this one was just a little thing, it wouldn't possible be missed." She switched to brushing another section. "Don't know why we can't keep just a wee little one around."

Of course, I knew why Colby didn't allow cats in the house. She was deathly allergic to them, even in her Undead state. Which hardly seemed fair, but who said being Undead was fair?

"Cheer up," I told her. "Maybe she'll let you get a dog or something."

"Do you really think so?" Sophie brightened at the thought of getting something as large as a dog and smiled while she completed her task.

"All right, mum, I've finished with your hair now. Piper, I need to put Miss Ileana to bed." She sounded like an old-fashioned nursery nanny instead of a young maid of twenty-something but I took the hint.

"Colby?" Ileana called to me as I reached the door. "Let's

catch up when I awaken, just you and I. Maybe we could go for tea at that lovely new teahouse by PSU?"

I tried to hide my surprise. Ileana had never asked to do anything with me, ever. In general, she tended to keep her distance with everyone. I thought it had something to do with all those years of protecting herself. Colby just thought she was a snob.

"Sounds great."

"Excellent, I have Sophie running some errands for me tomorrow and I don't want to go without my afternoon teatime."

Somehow Ileana had a way of turning a nice invitation into an obligation to serve her, but I ignored it because I knew she would speak frankly about the Prophesy without Sophie in the room. Sophie might be a maid, but Ileana was very protective of her and wouldn't allow anyone to say things that upset her. Things like how their existence was coming to an end. I imagine it sort of put a damper on their daily routine.

Seven

COLBY

I have a soul. Full, intact, complete. My essence is the exact same as it was when I was alive. Which would probably explain why feeding was still as tough for me now as it was the first time I tried it. I knew it was necessary to survive but that didn't make it any easier to walk up to a virtual stranger and take a pint of O negative.

Full-bloods, on the other hand, were missing a piece of their soul. It was probably an evolutionary necessity. Aunt Chloe told me once that during World War II soldiers used the worst kind of epithets for the enemy. The way they talked around the camps and such, you would think the enemy armies were demons. It was a means to dehumanize the people you were ordered to kill.

I don't think I really understood that until I became a vampire. How do you take an eighteen-year-old soldier who's been raised in a moral household where he was taught right from wrong and then expect him to put all that aside and kill another person?

I wasn't raised to drink other people's blood. But I have to do it or I die. And it's hard. Really hard. If I didn't have the support of others like me, I don't think I could keep doing it. I think eventually it would warp me. So full-bloods had to change. To evolve. To lose a bit of their humanity in order to survive.

I knew Thomas was not the same man he was when he was living. He's still a good man. He's just harder somehow, less sentimental, with more of an edge. He was missing a piece of his soul, his essence. To hunt your former peers, you must change. And he did.

I doubted Barnaby would come after me directly, but he needed me so he could play on the fears the Prophesy exacerbated. It was logical to assume he would come after someone close to me. That left two likely candidates. Thomas and Piper. And Piper had a complete soul. I wasn't totally ruling her out because Barnaby had unleashed his possessed playthings on us in the parking garage. At the time I thought they were only after me, but what if they weren't? After all, I didn't get staked and they'd tried to block the exits so Piper couldn't escape. If they only wanted me, who cared about a human girl getting away?

But if they killed Piper and possessed her body, they could try to influence me through her. But was she the logical first choice or were they getting desperate? Did they think they were running out of time? Maybe possessing Piper was Plan B. If so, what was Plan A?

I thought of Thomas. He wasn't sleeping at night, he was edgy and doing things I wouldn't categorize as rational. Sending Carl away to New York City was one such decision. Why send away his best friend when he knew we needed him here? Thomas was isolating himself. Not a good sign.

I returned to Psi Phi House and went directly up to my room. Would Thomas be there? Slowly, I opened the door so I wouldn't disturb him if he were sleeping. I was surprised to find him watching television, propped up on my bed.

"Hey," I said carefully. We were fighting the last time we spoke.

"Hey." He smiled his sleepy, sexy half-smile and my heart melted. He looked rested, like he'd finally gotten a decent rest.

"You look better." I shut the door behind me and joined him on the bed.

He reached out and drew me near, fitting our bodies together nicely. I sighed in contentment.

"I feel better. I haven't been able to sleep much lately—all these crazy dreams—but for some reason, I lay down here and was out. A good three hours of deep sleep. I feel like a new man."

"Did you get something to eat?" I asked, craning my neck back to look at his face. The dark circles seemed lighter, his muscles were less tense. Maybe he wasn't in danger of being possessed by a demon. Maybe he was just tired from all the extra work lately.

"I had a bag of A positive and it helped."

I wrinkled my nose up at him. "You can't be serious."

"It's really not that bad. It was pretty fresh, from this afternoon, so it still had some kick; but in general, I think I prefer it straight from the source."

"I don't know what Aunt Chloe was thinking. I mean, I get that we are a bit suspicious and all. There are twelve of us now and we have to feed daily. Sometimes we're lazy, we don't like to leave the area to feed and the bloodmobile van is kind of an ingenious way to keep the girls from eating out and risking exposure but still . . ."

"Ballsy," Thomas agreed.

"Yeah. Half-bloods just aren't as picky as you full-bloods. Guess we're not blood connoisseurs," I teased him.

He laughed at me. "Yeah, that's it." We looked into each other's eyes and I knew there was nothing I wouldn't do for this man. I was in love. Big-time.

He picked up my hand and laced his fingers through mine. "Look, about earlier . . ."

"Forget it. I'm sorry," I interrupted him, enjoying the feel of his hand in mine.

"Things have been hectic lately and I haven't really been able to spend enough quality time with you. I'd never want you to think that I only wanted you for one thing."

He was referring to my blood of course, which made me

laugh because prior to Thomas, guys used to be interested in a different thing.

I nuzzled his neck and kissed his ear. "Yeah, but my blood is pretty high-quality stuff."

He turned to look at me, moving his hand to hold my chin and keep me still.

"I love you, Colby."

It wasn't the first time he'd said it but it was the first time he was so focused about it. I wondered at his intensity. Dropping a quick kiss on the hand beneath my chin I replied, "Damn straight."

He smiled and that dimple that drove me crazy appeared and before I knew it, we were in a pretty passionate embrace. When he was done showing me exactly how much he loved me, we curled up together and Thomas fell asleep. Big shocker, right?

Admittedly, I was feeling pretty drowsy as well, but my mind refused to slow down. It kept racing with thoughts of the Prophesy, what I'd learned about demons and my concerns for Thomas.

"I'm always amazed how much he feels for you," I heard a voice say next to me.

I looked at Thomas and was surprised to find him awake. Except, it wasn't my Thomas. His eyes were aglow with red and rimmed with black. As if lined with eyeliner, as per Johnny Depp in *Pirates*. His voice was different as well. It sounded synthesized. This could only be Barnaby.

I pulled away, but he held me quick. I had, after all, fallen asleep wrapped in Thomas's arms.

"Oh no, don't go. I want to smell you." He took a deep sniff and I had to say, "Eww."

I still struggled but it was pointless. Thomas was strong but possessed by Barnaby, it was like being held by steel bands.

"You're not real. You'll never take over Thomas completely. You might manage it in his sleep, but he'll fight you."

I felt pretty stupid making that prediction because I was struggling and fighting him as well and I was hardly winning.

He laughed harshly and squeezed tighter. "I'm giving you the world and still you fight me. We'll rule together. You're so ungrateful."

He squeezed tighter until I cried out. My ribs cracked.

"Please," I begged and he immediately slackened his hold.

"You see, I'm not unreasonable, my pet. It's almost time to fulfill the Prophesy and you can take your rightful place as my queen. Imagine how the full-bloods will fear you." Then he nuzzled my cheek, sniffing again. Then he surprised me by licking my neck.

"I will have you," he promised, then savagely bit me. I gasped in pain and struggled, but he held me tighter and tighter. I couldn't move. My body was being smothered by his.

Suddenly the weight lifted. I sprang up in bed and a strangled cry escaped me in the dark room. I grabbed at my neck. It felt fine. No marks, no wetness from blood. I looked at Thomas next to me. He was quiet, sleeping peacefully. His face was relaxed and his hair brushed across his forehead in disarray. He looked so peaceful.

I tentatively reached out and touched him, relieved it was only a bad dream. He mumbled something and rolled over. My eyes went to the spot on the pillow his face occupied moments before. I stared at it for a long time, slowly inching away from Thomas to reach for my clothes. I couldn't stop looking there.

I touched my neck again and blinked away tears. His pillow was stained with blood and when I slipped out of bed, my ribs ached.

Eight

PIPER

Tea at ten P.M. masquerading as afternoon tea was something only the British and the crazy do. Ileana Romanav was both.

We settled down with our Earl Grey and lemon (Ileana ordered for both of us) in front of the fireplace to chat.

"I want you to know I still don't take much stock in the Prophesy." She sipped her tea delicately. "However, I know many Undead do and for that matter, it should not be taken lightly."

This was in direct conflict with her original position.

"You play it down to make Sophie feel better. That's a pretty decent thing to do."

"I play it down because it should be played down. And we don't need everyone in the House speculating and gossiping about something they can't change."

I looked around the teahouse and noted a few students, and possibly one professor. "What did your father believe?"

She sighed wearily. "He believed the Prophesy was true. He believed there was more to it than the obvious. However, he didn't believe it meant the end of vampire existence, but a unique opportunity for vampire evolution." She took another sip of her tea then added, "He thought vampires were noble, misunderstood creatures who should be idolized and worshipped."

"Was he crazy?" I had to know if she thought he was. I'm not sure I could believe my dad was crazy, even if he talked about nutty things. I guess I would live in denial and call him eccentric.

"He was a zealot. A strong believer who could never be convinced with logic or examples that his faith was misplaced. I imagine he thought he'd done something to bring on the attack that killed him. That it was his fault his precious Undead were ripping him apart, limb from limb. He'd done nothing but serve them."

I shivered at the image she evoked. "So you don't think any of his journals are worth reviewing?"

"No, what I'm saying is take anything in those things with a grain of salt, Piper. Zeal is one thing. A passion for your calling is not bad. When your passion clouds your judgment and common sense, it's time to step back and listen to a more objective opinion. I'm afraid there isn't much objectivity in those journals."

"So you've read them?"

She studied me quietly before answering, "Yes."

Just then Hunter arrived at the teahouse. I wasn't sure how he'd found me but the guy was like a bloodhound on a trail or something.

I introduced him to Ileana and he took the chair opposite our couch without invitation.

"I thought I'd find you here," he said without any hint of what had transpired between us earlier. He wasn't acting the least bit freaked out about our breaking-and-entering job the night before.

"My, what a well-built man you are, Hunter. Pray, what do you do to keep in such excellent shape?" Ileana practically purred in his direction as I shot daggers at her.

Hunter seemed flustered and a blush crept up his neck. My cool, alpha male was letting Ileana castrate him. "Stop it, Ileana," I said.

She turned her intense gaze on me and Hunter seemed to slump for a moment. She was using her vampire voodoo.

"Be careful with this one," she warned as she stood up and swept away from us.

My mouth fell open at her abrupt departure but Hunter's reaction surprised me more.

"Why are you here all alone?" he asked, after pulling himself together.

"Alone?" I said, doubtful I'd heard him correctly.

"Yeah, alone. You were just sitting here on the couch

when I sat down." He looked at me like I was crazy. Ileana had wiped the memory of meeting her from his mind. Nice trick.

"Can't a girl have a little tea and solitude?"

"How about tea and company? I think I found someplace we can find more of your special script."

"Really?" I was surprised he was still willing to help me. Heck, I was surprised he was still willing to see me.

"Did you get in okay?"

"Yeah, sure. You dropped me off right at the front door," I reminded him.

"Yeah, but I didn't see you go in the house and wanted to make sure everything was okay."

That was weird, but sweet of him to ask.

"I'm good. Fine. Where do you want to take me?" He stood up and I took his lead.

"Nope, no questions until we get there."

"Great, does that mean I get to drive?"

He looked horrified at the thought. Nope, I didn't think so.

*   *   *

It was a quiet destination.

"Why are we here again?" I asked Hunter, looking over a rather large and impressive headstone.

"I thought we might find some pagan symbols."

"Why this cemetery, in particular?" I jumped nimbly to the next headstone. I wasn't about to step directly on anyone's final resting spot. I knew enough Undead to be more respectful than that.

"Over there, past that fence, is the oldest part of the cemetery. It has a section of very interesting occupants."

He wiggled his dark brows.

"Define interesting." I glanced back in the direction he indicated.

"Suspected witches, zombies, vampires." He flashed a grin at me.

"You believe in that kind of stuff? Witches, vampires, zombies?" I mocked him, knowing in my heart that all three were quite real.

"Don't you?" he asked.

"Uh, no." I lied, following him to our destination. Once I stumbled. He grabbed my hand to steady me and just didn't let it go. His grip was strong, powerful and very warm. For a moment I thought of Carl's cool grip but the heat from Hunter's hand banished the memory. I needed someone alive and breathing. Carl needed someone like him.

"Why not?"

"Ever met one?" I asked.

"Every Halloween," he assured me.

"You know, I can dress up like a doctor but that doesn't mean I can perform open-heart surgery."

Hunter dropped my hand and pulled open his duster to reveal a muscular chest hugged by a tight black T-shirt. "I'd let you."

My heart skipped a beat but I kept my voice steady. "Then you *are* just another pretty face."

I'd turned the tables on him and he laughed at my joke. "Funny girl." He took my hand again.

"Any reason we had to visit this place at night?"

"Because you aren't available during the day?" he ventured. He'd never seen me during the day, so obviously he assumed I was too busy then. The truth was I kept unusual hours since my friends were Undead. It meant I stayed up at night and slept during the day, much like they did, but it didn't mean I thought traipsing around a cemetery at night was a good time.

"True, it's just kind of creepy here at night. What with the mist hanging over the graves like in a very bad horror movie."

"I'll protect you," he assured me.

But I had to remind him, "That is what every big, strong man says right before they get hacked up, sawed in half or eaten alive. They always leave the damsel to fend for herself and she ends up getting raped by a tree or something." Okay, maybe I'd seen *Evil Dead* one to many times. I can't help it. I love Bruce Campbell.

"But you don't believe in things that go bump in the night."

I stopped, effectively pulling my hand from his grip. He was throwing me off balance with all the flirting. It was time to do the same.

"I go bump in the night. Are you afraid of me?"

He stepped toward me.

"Should I be?"

We stood toe to toe in the mist, the world utterly silent around us. Was I really going to kiss Hunter for the first time *in a graveyard*? I could almost hear Colby's voice mocking me, "That is so *you*, Piper."

"Maybe *you* should be afraid of *me*?" He said it softly. I put my hand on his chest, where he offered to let me perform surgery earlier.

"Warm skin, strong heartbeat." Boldly taking a step forward so we were practically one shadow, I leaned in and gave his chest a soft kiss. Then I slid my hand up to his neck and gently touched the vein pulsing at its base with my index finger. His jaw clenched but he didn't move away.

"Steady pulse. Lifeblood." I stood on my tiptoes to kiss the pulse under my finger was. He sucked in a gulp of air. I paused a moment, wondering what I was doing. I'd never been this bold in my life but with Hunter, I wanted to be the aggressor. I wanted to kiss him. He was so confident and in control all the time that I wanted to be the one calling the shots for once.

I could barely reach the base of his throat with my lips. He wouldn't lean down to help me so I stretched a little more, my hands on his shoulders for balance. His neck radiated heat and I gave him the sweetest, smallest kiss on the throat.

I dropped down from my toes with a shy smile and looked up into his eyes.

Never had I seen a more frightened-looking guy than Hunter at that moment.

"What's wrong? What happened? Is there someone behind me?" I whipped around to see what terrible thing had crept up on us while Hunter was mesmerizing me, but we were totally alone.

Hunter gulped once, then again. He didn't move an inch, just kept staring down at me with the same fear and awe on his face.

"I can't fight you, Piper. I know you've hypnotized me and I know I can't stop you but I want you to know I—I want this. I want to give you what you need. It's against everything I believe but for you, I would do it."

It was a lovely speech, it really was. Very ardent and sincere. I just didn't have any idea what he was talking about.

"Huh?"

He pulled the neckline of his tee, actually ripping it away from his shoulder, exposing lots of tanned flesh. Wow, that was so hot.

"Don't hold back. I'm not afraid. Not of you. I know why I was called here now."

Yes, I was confused. Yes, I should have done the right thing, the decent thing, by making Hunter backpedal and explain himself fully. But the most amazing, sexy, gorgeous guy I'd ever met had just ripped his shirt practically off, exposing his hard muscles and begging me not to hold back and telling me how much he wanted me. Well, you would kiss him first and ask questions later too. Trust me on this one. You totally would. So I did.

I kissed his neck again, using my tongue to taste its saltiness. I kissed up his jawline and slid my hands up to his face, pulling it down so I could reach his lips. He resisted me for a moment, as though confused. Then he kissed me. We went straight to openmouthed kissing and Hunter was the perfect kisser. Not too slobbery, not too dry. He even sucked on my lower lip a little. Zowee.

I didn't have the experience with guys that Colby did, but I'd kissed a few of them here and there. It was nothing like kissing Hunter though. Kissing Hunter made time stand still. I couldn't form coherent thought, and no guy had ever done that to me before.

"Well, look what we have here. Two kinky lovebirds doing it in a graveyard."

We jumped away from each other in an instant. Were we being busted by some cemetery rent-a-cop? I looked around and couldn't see anyone. Something moved to my right and I was surprised to find a black cat sitting on a large gravestone, grooming itself. A black freakin' cat in the graveyard. Are you kidding me?

The cat put its paw down and looked quizzically at us. "Don't let me interrupt. Continue."

I was shocked. Did this cat just talk to us?

I grabbed Hunter's arm and pulled. He was staring at the cat too, but not in shock. More like annoyance.

"Chill, Hunter, it's not like the dame can hear me. She's a curvy one. You got good taste, man, but then you always did."

Hunter's expression went from annoyance to anger. Yes, the cat was talking. Except they didn't seem to think I could hear the talking cat. Because really, *that would be crazy*, right?

"Hunter? Why is that cat talking to us and why can I hear it?"

I'm not sure who was more surprised, Hunter or the cat.

"You can hear me?"

"You can hear him?"

They both spoke at the same time.

"Uh, yeah. Why is the cat talking?" I was trembling and Hunter immediately pulled off his duster and wrapped it around me. I couldn't seem to stop shaking. He pulled me close to him and we sank down on the grass. He rocked me in his arms and I tried to stop shaking.

"Chick's in shock, man," the cat proclaimed, jumping from the headstone to the grass.

"If you even think about crawling up in her lap and purring I will snap your scruffy neck here and now."

Hunter's face was thunderous. The cat paused in mid-step. He sat his furry bottom down a good five feet away from us and waited.

My shaking started to subside. The racking turned to tremors and the cat went back to licking himself. This time he was more industrious with his cleaning, deciding all his manly cat parts needed a thorough washing.

"Ew, do you have to do that here? Now? Have you no re-spect for the dead?" It had to be said.

"We-ll, lookie who's all proper now. I wasn't the one just exchanging slobber with a Demon Slayer in this oh sacred of sacred places, honey."

"Demon Slayer?" I repeated blankly, looking at Hunter. He was a Demon Slayer? What did that mean anyway?

"Well, you're the half-blood Protector," he blurted in his defense.

"She's not the Protector."

"I'm not the Protector."

The cat and I spoke in unison.

Hunter looked confused, then angry. "You have to be. I was under your spell. You *hypnotized* me!" he accused. "I was helpless to stop you from biting me and making me your Undead slave."

His tirade ended a bit lamely as though once the words were spoken he could hear how ridiculous they sounded. Hunter was still confused, but the cat thought it was hysteri-cal. He howled with kitty laughter.

"Oh my, oh my." He wiped tears of laughter from his eyes with his paw. "Oh, I can't stand it. Wait 'til the cats on the fence hear this one. Hunter falls for a girl he thinks is a vampire—and not just any vampire, but the one prophesied to bring the end of the world. Hahahaha."

I frowned at the cat. Hunter knew about the Prophesy? Then it clicked. Of course he did. That's why he was "helping" me. He thought I was the Protector and he wanted to see how I was going to end the world. I should have been furious, but the idea wasn't so far-fetched.

After all, I wouldn't meet him during the day. The Protector was my best friend and the first time we met she was injured. If he saw me stake that last vampire, it would be easy to assume I was the one who did all the slaughtering. Plus he had gone to a vampire sorority house to find me after seeing the Psi Phi House bumper sticker on my car.

I thought back to the vampire library, when he didn't seem at all surprised by all the weird stuff around him and when the alarm went off and the bright sunlight burst over us, he quickly threw his coat over me in an act of protection. Then he tried to get me to the House before dawn and even asked if I made it inside okay. It was a very chivalrous gesture, if he thought the sunlight would burn me to death.

And tonight he'd been willing to let me bite him because he wanted me so much. Sure, he thought I had hypnotized him, but I couldn't possibly have done that so he just really wanted me to kiss him. He liked me despite the fact that he thought I was a vampire. Obviously he'd struggled with this attraction a great deal, and he didn't need some mangy cat laughing at him for it.

I kicked out at the feline. "Knock it off."

The cat dodged my foot and I barely grazed its tail.

"No need to get physical, sweetie. It's just funny is all. If you knew Hunter like I knew him."

"I don't understand how you're not the Protector," Hunter protested. "I was so sure. I saw you kill that possessed vampire in the parking garage. You live in a vampire sorority house and you only come out at night. You dress all in black and you're so pale . . ."

"Hold on there. I don't look like a vampire, first of all. I have always been this lovely shade of alabaster and I happen to like the color black. It's very slimming. Second, I don't live at Psi Phi House, my friends do. I just hang out there. And finally, yes, I did take out one vampire in the parking garage, but staking one vamp does not a Protector make, get it?"

"But you hypnotized me," he repeated weakly.

I shook my head at him. "No, I didn't."

He seemed to absorb that statement then blurted, "Then who are you?"

I scooted away from him a little. "Who am I? I'm the same person I was thirty seconds ago. The same person you were kissing. Is the fact that I'm a normal human girl going to change things for you? And what's your beef with the Protector anyway?"

"Piper, I'm sorry. Give me a second to get things clear. I'm thrilled you're a normal, living person. Really, I am. More than you know." He grabbed my hand in his, slightly mollifying my anger. "But the Protector is another matter. She's going to bring upon the end of the world."

"Okay, I've had it with this stupid Prophesy! Enough is enough. Listen, I know the Protector. And she couldn't bring about the end of existence if she wanted to. She's not that kind of girl, okay? She's sugar and spice and everything nice and except for staking the occasional vampire who's out to get half-bloods, she's a very peace-loving person."

"But the Prophesy . . ."

I jumped to my feet and glared down at Hunter and the cat.

"Screw the Prophesy. The Prophesy is *wrong*. Did you ever consider that? Just like you were wrong about me, the Prophesy is wrong."

Hunter stood up to face me. "Piper, I wish I could believe you. I wish I had the luxury of believing everything is going to be okay, but I don't. I've seen too much and know too much to do that. Your friend is going to bring about the end of existence as we know it and I've been sent to stop her."

"What do you mean, you've been sent? Who made *you* the boss? Vampires don't answer to you. They have their own Council."

Hunter sat heavily and pulled me down to join him. I resisted for about three seconds. I guess if we were going to have a long chat in the graveyard, it was best to be comfortable. The cat went back to licking himself, which I pointedly ignored.

"Piper, I'm a Demon Slayer. My father was a Demon Slayer, my grandfather was a Demon Slayer and his father before him, et cetera, et cetera. I come from a long line of Demon Slayers."

I waited expectantly for more and when he didn't continue I said, "So?"

"So? So it's my duty to protect the world from demon invasion."

The cat stopped licking itself and looked up, suddenly interested in what Hunter was saying.

I pointed out the obvious. "But vampires aren't demons."

"No, they're not demons but they're susceptible to possession. For centuries vampires have been prey to demons."

"I don't understand."

"Piper, this is a demon." Hunter pointed to the cat.

"Are you saying all cats are really demons?"

"No, I'm saying *this* cat is a demon."

I shook my head at Hunter and the cat stuck his tongue out at me. Then he whipped it upward to try and pick his tiny cat nose with it. Blech.

"Animals don't have souls. Demons can possess animals. They just don't like to."

I watched the cat go back to licking himself. "I can see why."

"The only reason demons possess an animal is to try to get close to an ailing human, so they can slip into the body once the essence, or soul, leaves. The window of opportunity is very small. Once in a human body, the demon can survive until the natural decomposition of the body makes inhabiting it impossible," Hunter explained.

"Okay, so say Kibbles here jumps into a human body at

the right time. He can walk around and fake it for a little bit, but then people start to get suspicious when things get smelly and body parts start falling off?"

"In a nutshell, yes."

"Then what?"

"Then the demon is forced to leave the body. Much like how air escapes a balloon once the balloon is popped."

I made a face at the whole balloon-popping analogy.

"And there are different types of demons. Not all want to inhabit human form. Some are content to be cats forever, like Kibbles here." Hunter referenced the cat, who continued to ignore us. "Most are perfectly happy in their own plane of existence. They don't want to leave. But once in a while, a demon comes along who isn't satisfied with the status quo. They want more. They're ambitious. They get the other demons riled up by talking about dominating other planes of existence, like ours."

"I take it there is just such a demon making the rounds right now?" I eyed the cat suspiciously.

"Yes, and that isn't him. This is a Sloth Demon. They are perfectly content with their lot in life. Actually, as the name suggests, they really don't work too hard to change things. This cat has been in our world for a very long time. He inhabits the body of a new cat whenever his old one, well, retires. How many years have you been hanging around now?"

The cat looked at us with glowing eyes and said, "I'm not talking to you if you're gonna keep calling me Kibbles. You know that's not my name and not using it is disrespectful, I tell ya."

Hunter gave him a pained expression, "Fine. *Mr. Whiskers*, how long have you been a cat?"

"That's better. I've been a cat for fifty-seven human years. I've inhabited eleven cat bodies, all alley, except that mix-up in '64 when I was Siamese. Life as a house cat, of all things. It was embarrassing, I tell ya."

"If you're a Demon Slayer, why don't you just bash Mr. Whiskers in the head, right now?"

The cat screeched and hissed at me.

"Because this cat isn't a threat. He has no desire to inhabit a human form. He likes being a cat. He's harmless and he lets me know the word on the street."

"So this demon is harmless and you let it go on its merry way, but the Protector is some evil mastermind who is going to end the world and therefore must be destroyed. Even if I tell you she's perfectly harmless, like this cat?" I said.

"The difference is your Protector can be possessed by a very powerful, vicious demon bent on destroying the world and this cat will never be able to do that. Because it's still just a cat. But the Protector isn't as benign as a cat, is she? Now do you see my problem?"

It was a legitimate problem, I had to give him that. Colby on her own would never destroy the Undead community, but Colby possessed by some ambitious, Tony Robbins–type demon might have a shot. It could use her to create havoc within the vampire world and everyone would start turning against everyone else. But there were still things I needed to understand.

"What makes a vampire susceptible to possession?"

"Hah! Answer that one, smarty-pants." Mr. Whiskers tossed his ears back.

"Uh, well, I don't really know that," Hunter replied.

"What? Why not?"

"Because more than two hundred years ago vampires formed a self-governing body to protect themselves from extinction. They started patrolling themselves. They didn't need us anymore. Any demon possessions were dealt with internally. They were doing a great job monitoring their own and we had other demons to deal with, so, as each generation of Demon Slayer had less contact with vampires, the need to know how they could be possessed sort of died out."

"No one thought to write it down?" I couldn't help the sarcastic quality of my voice. But it sounded pretty irresponsible to let that kind of information disappear.

"Of course we wrote it down. All demon knowledge is categorized and written down. The information is kept safe, hidden."

"So where is it now?"

"Destroyed. All of it. Along with the Demon Slayers who guarded its secrets."

I noted the tenseness of his shoulders and how he clenched his jaw. He was a statue, wrapped in his pain.

"It was your family's duty, wasn't it? Your grandfather who studied ancient pagan scripts? He was a retired Demon Slayer in charge of the archives, wasn't he?"

Hunter gave me a brief nod and my heart went out to him.

"When did this happen?"

"Not long ago, six weeks. I was away and when I returned I learned my family had died in a fire. The police blamed faulty wiring in the kitchen. Our home was quite old, but I know it wasn't the wiring. It was arson. The archives were under the house, protected in stone catacombs. There is no way the fire could have gutted beneath the house unless someone deliberately set it in there as well."

"Hunter, I'm so sorry." I put my head on his shoulder and squeezed his arm.

"That framed text in the library, the one that was etched? I believe it was etched from the archives. Who made that etching, Piper? That person is responsible for the fire that killed my family."

"I don't know, Hunter. All I know is that display is new. It was just moved in the day we looked at it." I thought about the room a moment. "What about the other symbol? The one on the wall you got so mad about? What does that mean?"

After a moment's hesitation, Hunter pulled off his T-shirt. At first I thought it was a trick of the moonlight, the way the symbol on his chest flashed silver and black, but his tattoo had an iridescent quality that seemed to shimmer. It was the same symbol we'd seen on the wall.

I traced it with my finger. "What does it do?"

He shivered under the coolness of the night or the soft touch of my finger, I couldn't be sure. "It protects me from demon possession. A demon can never enter this body, even as my essence leaves, as long as I wear this symbol."

"If you lived in the house over the archives, how come you don't know how a demon possesses a vampire?"

"I've been gone a long time. I was fostered out to another Demon Slayer and was supposed to return home to finish my training and take over the ancient archives. But I . . . I left."

"I don't understand. What do you mean you left?"

"I mean I quit. I didn't want to be a Demon Slayer. But I'm a Legacy. I have no choice and I wanted, well, I wanted a choice." He looked ashamed of himself.

"I'll find out about the etchings. I promise. I'll find out who did this to your family and we'll stop them," I vowed.

"The only way to stop them is to tell me who the Protector is, Piper. That is the only way."

I felt like screaming, crying and running away all at once. I couldn't tell Hunter that Colby was the Protector. As far as Hunter knew, it could be anyone at Psi Phi House and I had to keep it that way. Colby was my best friend. She would not bring about the end of our existence, she just wouldn't. Demon or no.

"What I want to know," the cat interrupted us without preamble, "is how come she can hear me talk?"

We frowned at him. "You mean not everyone can hear

you jabber on when you're not licking yourself? Gee, lucky me," I said.

"Now don't be getting mad at me. It's not my fault your boyfriend here wants to kill one of your little friends. I just wanna know how come you can hear me."

"I'd like to know that as well." Hunter looked at me in question.

"How the hell do I know? It's the first time I've ever heard a cat talk, I can tell you that."

"Can you sense demons, girl?" the cat asked.

"Uh, no. This is the first time I've ever heard of demon possession. Duh."

"Is it?" Hunter asked. "Remember when we first met? You said you staked the last vampire. Do you fight vampires often?"

It was a trick question and I didn't want to give too much away. "Well, Psi Phi House is a sorority filled with half-blood vampires and there are many full-bloods who don't agree with the new laws giving them equal rights and emancipation. Since they're my friends I have been privy to an attack or two."

I hope that was just enough information to appease his curiosity without having to share any more details.

"So, you've seen a vampire die before?"

I thought back to the first time I watched a vampire die, the rogue who'd changed Colby. He'd tripped over me onto a picket fence and basically staked himself. It wasn't a pretty sight: He sort of melted until there was nothing left.

"Yes, I've seen it before."

"Was the garage different? Did it seem unusual to you?"

I snorted at his definition of unusual parking garage behavior. When Colby and I staked those vampires it was certainly different. They seemed to be decaying before we even touched them. Vampires are Undead, but they don't decay. They look perfectly fit. The one I staked smelled like sour milk and dissolved into foul-smelling goo. It didn't melt away into nothingness, like the first one.

"Yes, it was different. It smelled really gross. Like dairy gone bad and when the stake penetrated, there was a hissing sound. Like air leaving a balloon." I looked up in realization. "Ohmigod, do you think those vampires were possessed by demons? I mean demons other than the cat ones?"

"We're called Sloth Demons, you silly girl, Sloth. Sheesh."

I made a face at the cat. Now I knew why I was a dog person.

"How did you know they were coming? Could you smell them?" Hunter seemed very intent on what I had to say.

I tried to remember. "Well, let me think. We first noticed them in the food court, but we almost didn't see them at all. Then they were in the parking garage and they called out to us. Oh yeah, first they shot a crossbow bolt at us, that was nice," I added sarcastically. "Oh God, cramps."

"You have cramps?" Hunter asked, confused.

"No, I *had* cramps. That night. I noticed them at first in the food court, when I was eating. After that, I had them again, right before the bolt. I doubled over from the pain and the bolt just missed us."

I looked at Hunter for answers. What did this mean, anyway?

"Well, you're in luck, Hunter. It seems you've found yourself a cute little Huntress." The cat looked smugly over his shoulder, his tail swaying left and right.

Did he just call me a Huntress? I couldn't be a Demon Slayer. I just couldn't.

"I am so not a Huntress or Demon Slayer or whatever," I told them both. "There's no way."

"No one is saying you're a Demon Slayer." Hunter glared at the cat and tried to calm me down.

"Oh, but he is saying that, aren't you?" I directed my freaking out at the cat.

"Pretty much," he replied.

I jumped up and started pacing back and forth. "Oh no. No way. You're trying to trick me into revealing who the Protector is. I'm not going to do it. She's harmless!"

I was officially freaked now. I thought I might even throw in some hyperventilating, just for the heck of it.

"Damn it, Mr. Whiskers, why are you here anyway?" Hunter snapped, having completely lost control of the situation.

"Why, I have news, of course," the cat purred. "Barnaby is on the move."

I wasn't sure why Barnaby being on the move would be such major news to Hunter, but it was. I, however, was dealing with my own little crisis of possibly being a Demon Slayer so that kind of consumed my thoughts as Hunter interrogated the cat.

"Tell me everything," Hunter demanded.

"Not much to tell. I heard Barnaby made a little visit to your world today, via an unconscious mind. I don't know whose, but he must be getting ready for the full jump if he's making mini-visits."

Hunter grabbed me by the shoulders to get my attention. "Piper, you have to tell me who the Protector is. We are running out of time. Barnaby may have jumped into her body while she was unconscious or asleep. Tell me now."

I've never been one to cave to threats, so it was certainly the wrong approach to use with me. Hunter was desperate, I could see that, but I wasn't giving up Colby. Yeah, we fought but she was my best friend—and I knew in my heart of hearts she wasn't going to destroy the world. No matter what the fabulous-looking Hunter believed.

"No." Stubborn should have been my middle name. It's more fitting than Renee, that's for sure.

Hunter dropped his hands abruptly, but I noted they were clenched by his sides. He seemed coiled up, ready to strike out at the next thing he saw. I hoped the cat would say something but it wisely kept quiet.

"I'll find out if this Barnaby entered the Protector or someone around her." It was my idea of a peace offering.

"Or you could just tell me who the Protector is," he countered sarcastically.

I gave him a look that said it all.

"Why won't you trust me?" He was completely exasperated with me.

"Because if you knew for sure who the Protector was, you'd ride off into the sunset and kill her to stop the demon possession. I don't agree with that tactic so I am wisely keeping this information to myself."

"Don't you understand the world is at stake?"

"Don't you understand my best friend is at stake? Screw the Prophesy. I believe in her." There. The lines had been drawn. I had Colby's back, even if it meant losing Hunter.

We stared at each other in a showdown of sorts. He was the first to look away.

"You're loyal, I'll give you that."

He was backing down. I was kind of shocked. "Uh, thank you."

"Come on. I'll take you back to Psi Phi House."

Nine

COLBY

"Mr. Holloway said to give you anything you asked for."

The librarian looked positively ill saying the words. Instead of being snide, I thanked her.

Surprised by my attitude, she escorted me to the back room. "The exhibit just arrived. No one else has been allowed to see it yet. Here is an original copy of the Prophesy and a symbol found in a Demon Slayer archive."

"A what?" Surely I'd heard incorrectly.

"A Demon Slayer. Haven't you ever heard of a Demon Slayer?" The librarian had adopted her superior air again.

"No, would you tell me what a Demon Slayer is, please?"

I thought she'd fall over from shock. I'd actually asked her for information with a "please." I could almost see the wheels turning in her head: The Protector wasn't being surly. It was one of the signs of the apocalypse, what with the Prophesy so close at hand. Or something along those lines.

The truth of the matter is I'm rarely surly. Only to rude vampires, which she totally was, normally. But Mr. Holloway told her explicitly to give me anything I wanted so she was trying hard to comply. Had to give her props for that.

"A Demon Slayer is a person who slays demons."

I smiled tightly. Duh, I could have figured that out.

"Where do they live?"

"Unknown. Not a lot of them left anymore," she replied.

I looked at the symbol on the wall again. "It's sort of pretty, in a dark way."

She grunted at me. "Good riddance I say."

"Why?"

"Because Demon Slayers used to hunt vampires. That's why."

A good reason for a biased opinion, if I do say so myself.

"They used to? But they don't anymore?"

"During the founding of the Tribunal, a proclamation was sent to the Demon Slayers that all vampire matters would be dealt with by the new Vampire Investigators. Possessions, rogue vampire activities, half-blood creation—all those issues were now officially vampire jurisdiction only."

"You mean they weren't always?" I was surprised.

"No, demon possessions were dealt with by the Demon Slayers but other items in vampire society were given to them as well. It seemed"—she seemed to struggle with the right wording—"easier that way."

"Like, execution of half-blood vampires?" I tried to supply helpfully, with a minimum amount of sarcasm.

"Among other things. Look, Demon Slayers are no friends to full-blood vampires but I would think you, most of all, would have strong feelings about them."

"Why, because they used to kill half-bloods centuries ago? Full-bloods have done the same thing."

"What are they teaching you kids in college today? Don't you even take Vampire History 101?"

"It's on next semester's course load."

"Well, then you will discover that half-bloods found by a Demon Slayer were in for a fate worse than death."

"Why? What would they do?"

"What wouldn't they do? They used them as lab rats. Controlled experiments to record demon possession and test how long the process of full possession could take. They called it 'valuable research.'" She snorted. "Was it coincidence that vampire blood fetched a very high price on the magick black market? I think not; and even mongrel blood was better than none. That's how they funded their research."

"Let me get this straight. These Demon Slayers would invite demons to possess vampires, record how long it took, then drain their blood for profit to learn more about their trade?"

"Think the symbol's pretty now?" she questioned sharply.

I looked back at the artifact. "What does it mean?"

"It's the symbol of a Demon Slayer."

I stared at it long and hard. "Do you have texts or journals from the Demon Slayer's archive?"

She nodded. "A small amount survived the fire. The originals are coming in a different shipment. Being catalogued online first. I can get you access to them, if you want."

"I believe I would. Thanks for your help."

She grunted at me again, but quickly gave me access. I guess the old adage was true. You can catch more flies with honey than with vinegar. Now if it would only work with demons.

I had mixed emotions about reviewing the information found at the Slayer archive. I read about several half-blood experiments. The consensus among Slayers was that demon possession took three times as long with half-bloods as with full-bloods and then only after the subject had been exposed to large amounts of stimuli, aka torture. It seemed the weaker the subject was, the easier it was to possess.

The stark contrast was that while full-bloods could be in the best of health, possession could happen quickly if the vampire was reclusive and older. I thought of Thomas. Barnaby was slowly possessing him. I was sure of it. How long would it take? Thomas would fight him, but I knew I had to find a way to stop Barnaby. And quickly.

It was at that moment that I skimmed a passage that at first didn't seem relevant. But reading it planted a seed in my head. A tiny niggling idea that refused to quiet until I knew my brain was onto something big. I tried to put thoughts of Thomas out of my mind and focus on the task at hand.

I flagged down the librarian. "Where is the section on magick?"

As the daughter of a medical professional (and yes, orthodontists consider themselves part of the medical field) I was raised with a healthy respect for science. I always excelled in it at school and I loved the lab work. There was something about mixing chemicals together to get an entirely new compound that was pretty cool. I imagine it's what attracts witches to the potion profession.

Oh, excuse me. They weren't called witches anymore. They're called "Magick Engineers." They like being called witches about as much as flight attendants like being called stewardesses. Just an FYI.

I looked over several large volumes dealing with the history of magick in the vampire world but couldn't find what I wanted. I needed a *Magick for Dummies* sort of book.

"Is there anything about potions here? I want to know what sort of stuff vampire blood was used in."

The librarian gave me a startled look.

"No," I assured her, "I'm not planning anything sinister. You just mentioned that the Slayers would sell Undead blood on the magick market and I was wondering what it was used for."

She visibly relaxed when I explained myself. I wondered what sort of rumors my asking about the uses of vampire blood would spur but it couldn't be helped. Maybe some full-bloods would think twice about attacking me if they thought I would do something freaky with their blood.

"We don't have much here, unfortunately. We are, after all, first and foremost, a vampire library." She thought a moment. "You could check the PSU specialty library. They're online now. Mr. Holloway has given you full access so I can log you in."

"Really?" I had no idea my college had a specialty library dealing with magick. How would I know? I was studying Undead Living, not Hocus-Pocus for goodness's sake.

She moved to a different computer and signed me in. "Here you go. Just type in what you're looking for and it should give you a list of hits. Just like Google."

"Great."

I waited for her to take the hint and move on. She pouted once she realized I wasn't going to search in front of her but she did finally move away.

I entered "vampire blood" and had close to twelve hundred hits. Ugh. I certainly didn't have that kind of time. I added "magick" to the search and saw the list drop dramatically.

It was fascinating stuff, really. I thought of magick as a kind of voodoo but it was really more medicinal in origin. Sure, I stumbled across the occasional "love spell" crap but the primary use of vampire blood now was in creating a potion that reduced blood cravings so vampires wouldn't be overwhelmed with the need to hunt. Which can be especially tricky if you were trying to keep a low profile.

It was interesting, but not what I wanted. I doubted a Demon Slayer would use vampire blood for that purpose. I know the librarian thought they sold it to fund their research but I read some things that led me to believe they used the blood for their own purposes. Why use vampire blood? What benefits could it possible have to a Demon Slayer?

Several hours later I stumbled across the answer. Or at least, what I thought the answer might be. Vampire blood was used in potions to ward off other Undead, and could be used to protect a place or a person too. Demons fell under the Undead umbrella. Interesting.

I clicked a new link and gasped when the symbol from the back room in the library popped up. The one I thought was pretty. I read the description and was stunned. The symbol wasn't a Demon Slayer ID badge. It was a protective spell. It kept the Slayer's body from being possessed by a demon, even at the most vulnerable time. It required the use of vampire blood. I'd just found the solution to my problem.

Ten

PIPER

Hunter returned me to Psi Phi House. He wanted to come inside but I was having none of that. I promised I would call him as soon as I heard something and, reluctantly, he left. I needed to find Colby.

I entered the house to the usual chaos. Sage was pimping out her new elixir that very few people were willing to try. I think she added milk to the mix so I couldn't blame the gals from steering clear of her.

Aunt Chloe was at the dining room table, making her charts for the week. I plopped down beside her.

"Hello, dear. In a better mood today?"

That was a loaded question.

"Sorry I was so short with you, Aunt Chloe. Vampire attacks make me cranky." I took one of the charts from her pile and started to review it.

She chuckled. "They make me cranky too. Can't blame you a bit. Were you just out with your new feller?"

I dropped the chart. How did she know about Hunter?

She laughed again. "Can't keep secrets from me, Piper. I am the all-knowing housemother." She winked. "Besides, since the cataract surgery, I can see pretty far now. Its not too much of a strain to look out the dining room window and see a very well-built young man on a motorcycle."

Okay, so it didn't take Sherlock Holmes to figure out Hunter dropped me off on the back of his motorbike. For a minute there, she had me freaked out.

"Where did you two lovebirds go?" she wanted to know.

"Graveyard," I answered honestly.

She nodded in approval. "More original than catching a movie, and cheaper too."

Nothing fazed Aunt Chloe.

"Is Colby here?" I asked.

"I'm not sure, dear. She left to go to the library but she might be back by now."

I thanked Aunt Chloe and made my way upstairs to Colby's room. I met Thomas on the stairs. He looked awful.

"Dude, you look terrible." I was not known for my tact.

"Thanks, I feel terrible."

"Are you coming down with something? Can vampires get sick?" I asked. Thomas did indeed look like death warmed over. And considering he was Undead, that was a really bad look for him. The dark circles under his eyes highlighted how bloodshot they were.

He shook his head. "Have you seen Colby?"

"I was looking for her myself."

"I have to go to the office. If you see her, have her call me. Okay?"

"Sure," I watched him go down the stairs and out of sight. I wasn't sure what demon possession looked like but I had a sneaky suspicion Thomas could be the poster child. He had a hunted look that was uncharacteristic. I wondered if the guy had slept in the past week.

I needed to find Colby and tell her what I knew. But would I tell her everything? I wasn't sure. She wouldn't take it well that Hunter was not just some random guy but some-one with an agenda. She was right about that, which made me inclined not to tell her about him. She would throw that back into my face every time I doubted her judgment again. I was so not willing to pay that price.

I went to Colby's room to wait for her. I pulled out the Prophesy to see if I could make any sense out of it with my new information but it still seemed as random as it had before.

This time the mixed blood will rise,
The One who is Undead but Alive,
who is pure but not whole,
And they will bring forth the beginning of the end.

I was pretty sure I understood the first sentence. It referred to half-bloods earning rights and being allowed to live. They were considered mixed bloods or mongrels by full-bloods. They were too many generations removed from the original vampires and therefore too watered down to have all of the powers.

The second line could be interpreted as Colby. She was Undead but had many living characteristics because of her half-blood status. It was easy to see why full-bloods—and apparently Demon Slayers—thought she was the one in the Prophesy. She did emancipate the half-bloods, which could be seen as them "rising."

It was the last two lines that didn't make sense to me.

Who is pure but not whole,
And they will bring forth the beginning of the end.

Who was pure but not whole? Was that Colby or was it referring to someone else? Did "they" in the last line refer to Psi Phi House? Did it mean the half-bloods would bring the beginning of the end or was I missing something?

God, I hated this! I crumpled up the Prophesy and threw it in the garbage. I didn't need it written down. I had the stupid thing memorized. No matter how many times I reviewed it, things looked bad for Colby.

At that moment, she peeked in. I watched her in surprise as she surveyed the room, noted me and let out a sigh of relief.

"Okay, that was weird," I said to her.

"I was looking for Thomas," she confessed, closing the door behind her and plopping down on the end of the bed.

"You just missed him. He wants you to call him when you get the chance."

She made a face. "How did he look?"

"Awful. Is he sick or something?"

She fell back on the bed, feet dangling over the edge, and replied, "You have no idea."

I debated how to start the conversation with her. She looked so young lying on her fluffy, pink bed. She'd been changed into a vampire when she was seventeen and she still looked that age. We were both eighteen now, almost nineteen, but she didn't look as though she'd aged a day. I looked older but she would forever be seventeen. At least physically.

"I have some news," I ventured slowly.

"Really? Me too."

She didn't ask to hear it so I waited a moment then said, "Do you want to go first?"

"Sure, why not? There is some super über demon named Barnaby that is planning on taking over the world." She rolled over onto her stomach and hugged a stuffed princess crown pillow to her chest. "Oh yeah, and I think he's trying to possess Thomas to get to me to achieve his goals."

So, she did know what was going on. That was sort of a relief.

"You're taking it remarkably well," I said slowly. I'd

never seen Colby so detached before. She was usually all fired up and ready to tackle the world when injustice reared its ugly head.

"Am I?" She peered at me through lowered lashes. "So are you. I take it you have similar news to share?"

"I just knew about the demon part, not the trying to possess Thomas part."

"How'd you find out?"

I wondered if I should lie. Instead I said, "Talking cat told me."

She nodded like it was no big deal that a talking cat told me that a demon wanted to take over the world and pin it on her.

I stood up and moved toward her on the bed. "Colby?" I tentatively put my hand on her back since she'd buried her face in the crown pillow. Her shoulders shook as she sobbed.

Colby was crying. I started to freak out. Colby was the planner. The one who looked at all the facts and formulated an attack. She didn't break down and cry into a pillow.

I stroked her hair and let her sob a few more times. I reached toward the desk and grabbed a box of tissue. "You done now?" She took a moment but nodded.

"Good, because your eyes get all puffy and red when you cry and I know how you hate that."

She slowly pulled herself up into the seated position and reached for the tissue. She had no tears and her eyes weren't red. In fact, since she became a vampire, she always looked beautiful, morning or night. It was one of those things I guess. But it seemed to make things more normal if I talked to her like things were the same as they'd always been.

"What are you going to do?" I asked her.

She wiped her dry eyes. "I have no idea."

I raised an eyebrow in disbelief.

"The day you don't have a plan is the day the Prophesy actually comes true."

"Yeah, that did sound like quitter talk, didn't it?"

I nodded in agreement, feeling better as she started to rally.

"How are you going to stop the demon from possessing Thomas?"

She blew her nose. "Oh, I'm not."

"Huh?"

"I'm not going to stop it. I'm going to be right there when it happens."

"You're not planning on destroying mankind, are you?" I asked, half joking. I'd never seen Colby like this before.

"Hardly. I plan on trapping a demon."

"Oh, that sounds like a good plan. How are you going to go about doing it?"

"I'm a little hazy on the details."

I nodded. "All good plans take time to work out the logistics. Except, I don't think we have a lot of time."

She eyed me critically. "Exactly what did this talking cat say to you, anyway?"

"He said Barnaby was on the move."

Colby stared at me in stunned silence. Apparently, she hadn't been taking my talking cat story at all seriously.

"And then what?"

"Oh, that I might be a Demon Slayer because I got cramps whenever demon-possessed vampires were around."

"You might be a *what*?!" Her voice raised several decibels over that revelation.

"A Demon Slayer. Have you heard of them?" I was surprised, because I never had.

"You're telling me some cat thinks you're a Demon Slayer because of PMS?"

"Uh, no. I'm saying the cat thinks I'm a Demon Slayer because my uterus contracts whenever evil vampire zombies are in the room. Oh, and because I can hear him talk. He's really a Sloth Demon possessing a cat."

"*What*?!" she screeched again.

"Yeah, like that's any more far-fetched than you coming home a half-blood vampire who must defend her Undead existence."

Really, was it so hard to believe that I could be a Demon Slayer if she could be the half-blood Protector?

"I was attacked and missing for two days. I was turned into a vampire. You're saying you just woke up one day with an evil-sensing womb and the ability to speak to cats."

"Yeah, so? Maybe I didn't need an attack to change me. Maybe it was inside me all this time and didn't surface until I was ready to handle it."

She jumped to her feet. "Are you listening to yourself? You sound crazy!"

"*I* sound crazy? Have you ever listened to yourself? 'I was attacked again by full-blooded vampires.' Now that sounds crazy."

"But that's real. Those things happen," she tried to argue.

"And my being a Demon Slayer isn't real?" I said quietly.

"Can you prove it?"

"Can you prove you aren't going to bring forth the beginning of the end?"

She threw her hands up in disgust. "That is totally not the same thing and you know it."

I stood up to face her toe-to-toe. "No, it's exactly the same thing. It's called having faith. I believe you won't end the world so I believe the Prophesy isn't true. Even though countless others believe it so strongly they are willing to kill you or die for it. I believe in you so much that I am willing to gamble the world, but you won't believe in me when I say I'm a Demon Slayer who can talk to possessed cats?"

Colby wiped her face with both hands trying to grasp what I was saying.

"But it sounds impossible."

"No more impossible than vampires and zombies. But we now know they exist."

I was standing my ground. I believed in her. I had better because I was protecting her secret at the risk of destroying the world. Was it so much to ask that she believe in me too?

"No one has even seen a Demon Slayer in years."

I straightened my back to stand taller. "I'm a Demon Slayer."

And as I said it I knew in my heart that it was true. That was why Hunter and I connected. We were the same. We shared this bond. It was who I was, just like being a Protector was who Colby was and being a Vampire Investigator was who Thomas and Carl were.

"It's too much, Piper. I can't deal with this right now."

I looked around her bright and perky room. Colby was bright and perky but she was also dangerous and had killed. She could be all those things but I couldn't be a Demon Slayer?

"We need to work together on this, Colby. Barnaby is a real threat."

"Yes, I know it's a real threat. I'm not ignorant. I get the implications. But we are talking about Thomas here. I think I can save him and destroy Barnaby at the same time and I don't need some 'Demon Slayer' telling me how to be the Protector."

She referred to "Demon Slayer" with air quotes—as though I was pretending. As though I could add no value. Sometimes Colby really pissed me off.

"If you can get off your high horse long enough, you'll see I can help you with this. What if you can't take out Barnaby and he possesses Thomas for good? Can you do what needs to be done?"

She glared at me. "That's not gonna happen. But hey, the minute I need the insights of a talking cat, I'll give you a call."

I'd had enough. I stood up and left Colby without another word. She could be such a bitch sometimes. She never asked for help, always thought she could do it all and never thought about the repercussions of her actions.

The week she was attacked, she'd been warned not to walk home alone or at night but no, Little Miss Nothing Can Happen to Me did it anyway and was attacked by a rogue Vampire and turned into an Undead. Do you think she once thought it was a bad idea to walk alone? Noooo, she just moved forward without ever thinking her actions had consequences.

If she had swallowed her pride back then and called her parents to pick her up after Aidan took another cheerleader home, she would be a normal college student now. But she didn't want anyone to know she'd been dumped so she walked home in the dark. Like she was freakin' bulletproof or something.

Would she do the same thing now? Would she refuse to consider the ramifications if she failed to destroy Barnaby after he fully possessed Thomas? Once Barnaby crossed over, he could destroy the world as the Prophesy foretold. And it would be Colby's fault.

If she had to choose between Thomas and saving the world, would she do it?

For that matter, wasn't I doing the same thing? Could I be

called upon to do the necessary thing if things went wrong? I didn't know. And I was fairly certain Colby didn't know if she could either.

What I *did* know was Colby was making a plan. Great, we'd use that as Plan A. Hunter and I would come up with Plan B, in case Colby failed. That was rational thinking. I would prefer to work with Colby and share information, but it was obvious she wasn't going to let that happen. I couldn't very well introduce her to Hunter so they could collaborate. He might try to kill her.

It was hell when your best friend and your boyfriend couldn't get along. What was a girl to do?

Eleven

COLBY

I couldn't believe that Piper thought she was a Demon Slayer. Had she finally lost her mind? Was having me as a best friend so much pressure for her that she had to invent some elaborate persona to feel like she could compete?

Whatever it was, she picked a fine time to lose it. I could have used her help but now I would have to do everything on my own. I thought about enlisting aid from Thomas but what could I really tell him? "I think you're being possessed by a demon and I need your help to stop it?" What if Barnaby had access to Thomas's memories? It wouldn't help if the demon knew I had a plan.

Damn it, Piper. I really could have used your help! I needed someone to research the most likely time Barnaby would try to take full possession of Thomas so I could be ready for it. And I still needed to gather the right ingredients and find someone to create the symbol for me. That left using someone in the house. Someone who could be discreet and was used to keeping life-or-death secrets. It meant turning to Ileana. Oh, joy of joys.

I rummaged through my desk to find the journals she'd loaned me. I vaguely remembered something in one of the books about symbols. As I thumbed through them, I was again struck by how crazy her father must have been. He blindly followed his Undead "Masters," as he called them, convinced they were perfect and would honor him with immortality. Poor slob. He ran around doing their errands and bidding, only to be ripped apart when the vampires got a little peckish.

I had an uneasy feeling that there was a parallel between his story and my relationship with Piper but I pushed it away. It was so not even the same thing. Piper was my friend. And most of the time she didn't act like a loon. We helped each other. It was give and take. Not what Ileana's father had with his vampire "masters" at all.

I found the passage I was looking for with a triumphant "Aha!" Listed in the text was a ceremony requiring vampire blood as one of the magick ingredients. I read through the scene, trying hard not to *hrmph* the many references toward "The Exalted One" and his "Benevolent Masters." This was exactly what I was hoping to find.

I took the book with me to Ileana's room. She was reading and listening to classical music while Sophie softly hummed along, hemming a new pair of pants. Ileana shopped like most people went to work. She considered it her reason for being.

"Hi, there," I interrupted, pushing the door farther ajar than it was and stepping inside the room.

"Ah, so you've finally come have you?" Ileana announced, closing her book delicately and setting it aside.

"You were expecting me?"

She waved me toward the chair opposite hers. "Of course, though frankly I thought I'd see you earlier."

I joined her in the corner.

"Interesting reading, no?" she said, referring to the journal in my hand.

"Very educational."

She laughed at my attempt at tact. Her bright, luminescent eyes and perfect features schooled themselves into a pensive look. "A shame, really. Such devotion to such undeserving scoundrels. Even in life they were riffraff. Whatever made my father think that death would elevate them into perfection, I'll never know."

I wasn't sure what to say so I jumped right to the point. "Your father mentions a ceremony in this journal." I handed her the book. "How would I go about getting those ingredients?"

She reviewed the volume and gave me a calculating look.

"Risky, what you're considering." Then she abruptly turned her attention to her maid. "Sophie, be a dear and fetch me one of Sage's new concoctions, will you? I am feeling parched."

"Of course, mum." Sophie jumped to do Ileana's bidding and left the room.

"What if it doesn't work?" Ileana turned her attention back to me.

"Ah, a ploy to get Sophie to leave." I was relieved. "For a minute I thought you actually wanted Sage's drink."

She gave a small smile. "At times, I have found having some small acting ability is not without benefit. Now about the ceremony . . ."

"If it doesn't work, I will take care of Barnaby myself."

"Really? He will be quite powerful in our world and wield all the attributes of that whom he possesses." Her doubt had me second-guessing myself. I hated that.

"I can handle it."

We stared at each other a moment longer before she replied, "Let us hope for all our sakes you can."

Sophie returned with a glass of foul-looking pink liquid. Ileana took a sip and smiled at her maid. "Perfect; thank you, Sophie."

I had to admire her acting skills because I'd tasted the stuff and knew it to be awful.

"You will need these things." Ileana put the glass down and scribbled a list of ingredients on a sheet of notebook paper. She had beautiful handwriting, spiked and loopy at the same time.

She handed it to me.

"Where in the world do I find this stuff?" I didn't recognize most of the ingredients on the list.

She let out a labored sigh. "Sophie, those pants can wait. I have another errand for you." She yanked the sheet from my fingers and handed it gently to Sophie.

"You can find these things in the underground, beneath Pike's Place. You know the secret shop I am referring to? Beneath the comic book store?"

Sophie bobbed her head in affirmation.

"Tell Mira they're for me, you'll get the best price. Deliver them to Colby and our part is concluded."

I looked at Ileana in question. "But how do I . . . ?"

"I said our part in your plan is concluded. I can do no more."

I got up when she went back to reading her book and Sophie scurried out of the room. At the door, I turned back one last time. "Where will I find someone to mix it and, you know?" I made a jabbing motion.

"You need a Magick Engineer, at least a level four. Try Ms. Weatherbee at the college."

"But Ms. Weatherbee is my guidance counselor."

She looked up from her book in disgust. "Really, Colby, are you so self-involved you don't see the things around you?

Ms. Weatherbee is an accomplished Magick Engineer whose skill is greatly respected in the Undead community. She can help you mix it correctly but the"—she made the same jabbing motion back at me—"is up to you."

I muttered a thanks and slunk out of the room, properly chastised. Ileana did notice everything around her. She noticed whenever someone was wearing something new or had a different hairstyle. She even figured out that Lucy was a vampire spy and not an innocent half-blood, way before I pieced it together.

I looked at the time and wondered if Magick Engineers kept vampire hours. Probably not. I would have to wait until the sun came up and try to find Ms. Weatherbee at school. I might even catch a class or two. What a novel concept. This Prophesy was playing havoc with my schoolwork.

I thought about Piper and her claims but decided to dwell on it later. I couldn't get into that now. Should I call Thomas back? He'd been so sweet before he fell asleep, just like the man I fell in love with . . . and then that stupid demon had to ruin our time together. How long did I have until Barnaby made his move to full-time occupancy? A day? A week? Longer? I couldn't be sure. It seemed like it would be sooner rather than later if I could trust my gut.

I went downstairs in time to join a House meeting in full progress. Aunt Chloe went on about the new weekly lists. We praised Sage for losing two pounds and talked about the success of the blood drive. Apparently, we were actually able to give almost half of the blood to the bank. Yay us. It still felt creepy, but maybe it wasn't so bad. At least, I kept telling myself that.

Sophie caught me right as the meeting was ending and gave me a small brown bag. I thanked her and took a quick sniff of the contents. Blech.

I had just enough time for a quick snack before heading off to school. I passed Mrs. Murphy's house and when one of her cats spotted me, it let out a long, miserable yowl. Like it was trying to wake the dead or something.

I've got news for you kitty, I'm already up, I thought.

It began to follow me. Surely I was mistaken. It looked like the same calico I made Sage take back after Sophie "adopted" it. The last thing I needed was a pathetic hanger-on cat who wanted to be fed. I had to eat myself. I turned back to it.

"Shoo, cat. Beat it. I've got stuff to do today."

It stood still and stared at me with yellow eyes. I turned to walk and sure enough, the cat continued to follow me. *Stupid cat. Fine, follow me all the way to school. You're not my responsibility.*

I felt like a jerk walking ten paces in front of a cat who was walking in step with me. I decided to lose it at the Starbucks. I went in one side and tried to mix in with the throng of people waiting for their caffeine hit, then snuck out the side. I weaved around the back of several businesses and back out to a side street. I looked back. No cat. I'd lost it.

I was such a freak, taking the time and trouble to lose a cat that was probably just following the smell of coffee and cream to get food. Still, I did give it the slip so part of me was pleased with my ability to lose a tail. No pun intended.

I arrived on campus and made a beeline straight to Ms. Weatherbee's office. It was seven in the morning but I was hoping she taught an early class and would stop by her office first. Luck was on my side because I only had to wait ten minutes before she arrived.

She was of average height and size, dark hair pulled back with a barrette, juggling a briefcase, her coffee mug and a purse, while trying to find her keys. She looked like any professor on campus, probably in her thirties.

I jumped up to help her by taking the keys out of her hand and opening her door.

"Thank you, Colby. What a nice surprise," she said as she dumped her things on her chair and desk. "Do you need any scheduling help? Are you thinking about next semester so soon?"

She sat down in her ergonomic chair and took a sip of her latte.

"No, Ms. Weatherbee, I'm actually here to ask a favor," I replied.

She seemed surprised. "Really? Well, I'll certainly help if I can."

I handed her the list of ingredients and said, "I need help mixing these."

She tried to mask her surprise by making a great show of putting on reading glasses, which I suspected she didn't really need. They looked more for show than actual purpose. After reviewing the list, she looked at me with a new type of respect. Or a new type of disbelief, I couldn't be certain.

"Are you aware of what this is?"

"Yes, ma'am."

"Then you know how to administer it?"

"Sadly, I'm aware."

She nodded. "Who's going to do it?"

I took a deep breath. "Me, myself and I."

"It's best that way. Keeps the potion strong without diluting its purpose with another person's energy." She took stock of me for a moment then asked, "Colby, do you want some advice?"

I nodded. "Desperately."

She shot backward in her chair and turned at the last minute to fling open a filing cabinet. She removed a vial that glistened and moved like mercury.

"I suggest adding this to your mix."

"What is it?"

"Liquid silver. Aesthetically, it adds a nice shimmering quality to the potion; fundamentally, it will boost the potency, helping create a more solid symbol."

I nodded and she added it to my bag.

"So you know what I'm doing?" I blurted out.

"I have a sneaking suspicion. Do *you* know what you're doing?"

"Vaguely," I assured her with a half smile.

"Then what can possibly go wrong?"

We shared a nervous laugh together. She took my bag and placed each one of the ingredients on her desk. Among the things I could identify were small bags of herbs, a sort of paste, two rocks and a vial of dried black paint.

"Uh-oh," she said, opening the paint and sniffing it. "This won't work. It's dried." She looked at the receipt and shook her head in dismay. "This is a very reputable distributor. I'd bet they gave you their last vial. Without this, your potion will be useless. I'm so sorry, Colby." She seemed genuinely distressed to share the news with me.

"Can't I use a substitute or find it online?"

She shook her head at me. "How would you know it was pure if you bought it from some unknown source on the Internet? This is too important to risk that. No, you're going to have to come up with a Plan B."

I shook my head at her. "There is no Plan B. At least, not one I would seriously like to entertain. Please, is there anything I can do?"

She eyed me warily, visibly torn between doing what I asked and possibly protecting me. "All right, Colby. I'll help you. I can tell you where to find this last ingredient, but it's up to you to get the liquid equivalent, okay? You will need less if it's fresh." She riffled through the same file cabinet and gave me a vial. "About this much."

I nodded. "Where do I get it?"

"Close the door," she instructed and I hurried to comply. Something was about to happen. Something cool and mystical and I was going to witness it. I watched her pull out a phone book and drop it open on her desk. The pages fluttered, falling open to a yellow section. She closed her eyes and dropped her finger. She looked at the address and wrote it down, including a room number.

You have got to be kidding me. "That was magick in its greatest form?" I was incredulous.

She handed me the paper. "No, that was me, jerking your chain. I knew the address before you got here. I had a vision last night."

"Oh, good one." I was disconcerted. Ms. Weatherbee had a warped sense of humor and was actually pretty entertaining. I never even suspected.

"And Colby, if you hurry, you can be in and out with no one being the wiser. Come back tonight and we'll make your potion."

I had to ask, "Ms. Weatherbee? Why are you doing all this for me?"

She seemed surprised. "Because you asked for my help."

"Really? Just because I asked?"

"No, not really. Mr. Holloway instructed me to help you

in any way I could. It just made me sound pretty cool the other way, didn't it?"

I laughed at her again. She was actually a riot.

"One more thing. What am I getting, anyway?"

She became serious. "Blood. You're getting the blood of a Demon Slayer."

Twelve

PIPER

I decided to go to bed. When feeling overwhelmed, climbing in bed and hiding seemed the logical course of action. Of course, I couldn't stay in bed forever, but a nice long nap sounded heavenly.

Sleep came surprisingly quick. I was exhausted, but my mind had a hard time shutting off. I dreamt Hunter was being crushed to death by a demon and he was screaming my name. I had to help him but I did what I always did: I froze. He just kept calling to me and I couldn't move. I was stuck. Incapable of motion.

The dream constantly changed but the results were the same. I couldn't help because I was paralyzed with fear. I would be the worse Demon Slayer in history. It didn't take a talking cat to figure that out.

Depressed and feeling sorry for myself, I drove to the Psi Phi House. I called and left Hunter a voice mail to join me at the teahouse when he woke up. My best friend didn't believe I was a Demon Slayer and Hunter hadn't really jumped at the chance to confirm the cat's suspicions either. Apparently, the only creatures that believed I was a Demon Slayer were Mr. Whiskers and me. Hardly an auspicious beginning.

I parked about a block away from the House so I could walk around and get some air. I wasn't sure what I was going to say when I saw Colby. We'd had a fight, sure. But then, that's what we did. We fought. It wasn't like we couldn't work things out. She'd come around, eventually.

The weather was brisk for a spring morning, but I didn't mind. The cool air cleared my head. I noticed a small gray cat about two houses from Psi Phi House patiently waiting for me to approach, as though it was expecting me. I thought about Mr. Whiskers. Should I greet this cat and risk looking like an idiot when it turned out to be just another cat?

Suddenly, I felt a sharp pain rush through my stomach and I doubled over, therefore narrowly missing the sword that came swooshing at my head. I spun around behind one of the trees that lined the street, using it defensively. A very determined and fermenting vampire was swinging the sword at me for all he was worth, but the tree kept getting in the way.

I did what any self-respecting Demon Slayer would do. I screamed bloody murder. I was too far away from Psi Phi House for a regular person to hear me, but a half-blood who inherited super vampire hearing would have no problem. Were any of those at home?

My only other option was to break off a tree branch and stake my attacker. Did I mention he had a sword? It was unlikely I could get close enough with a piece of wood, even if I did manage to snap one off the healthy tree, without being stabbed or beheaded.

The vampire made another attempt with his sword, this time embedding it in the tree. It was my chance. I kicked him in the groin as he tried to pull the sword lose. The results were not pretty. At least not for him. My foot caught him in the upper right thigh and his leg snapped off at the hip. He tipped over, still trying to pull the sword out.

I tried to run past him, but he grabbed my leg with his hand and I fell.

"My master is coming for you, Demon Slayer," it rasped as I tried to kick loose. *See, even the vampire zombie knew I was a Demon Slayer, why couldn't Colby see it?*

He pulled me closer and I kicked again, this time making contact with his head, snapping it at the neck. When that didn't stop him from pulling me toward him I thought, *Enough is enough already.* I trapped his hand by crossing my legs together at the ankle and rolled, hard. The bones in his hand splintered and snapped until he couldn't hold on anymore.

I scrambled to my feet to run but faltered when I looked back. On the ground, looking much like a bad-smelling, skeletal Terminator, was the vampire zombie, still trying to get to me. I nimbly jumped out of his reach and yanked the sword from the tree.

"Nighty-night," I said right before severing his neck, effectively removing his head from his body. A hiss of white mist escaped the wound and dissipated into the thin air.

Proud of myself, I looked around to see who witnessed my heroic deed. That would be a resounding no one. Well, no one except the gray cat, who hadn't moved from his spot through the entire fight.

"Not bad for a newbie, eh?" I said in his direction as I sauntered toward Psi Phi House, brimming with self-confidence.

"Yeah, cutting down a decaying zombie is pretty hot stuff, Slayer."

The damn cat spoke to me.

"You know, you think it's easy being a Slayer? There you are in your safe little kitty body, drinking milk out of bowls and getting scratched behind the ears. I don't see anyone chasing you down with a sword." I so did not need any attitude from a Sloth Demon right now.

"Ever been chased by a dog? It's not all peaches and cream." It started walking beside me.

"I don't remember asking for an escort." I glared at him.

"I got news," the cat said.

"Find Hunter, he's the guy you want."

"Can't. Word on the street is the Protector's after him. She should be taking care of business right about now."

I stopped and demanded, "How do you know that?"

"I have my ways," he assured me mysteriously. I waved

the sword around menacingly. "Okay, fine. I'll spill. You Slayers are all so violent. I know a cat who hangs with a Familiar. Some teacher dame at the college is making up a potion for the Protector that requires Demon Slayer blood."

"What kind of potion?"

"Do I look like a magick encyclopedia to you?" He was indignant.

"Whatever, I have to go."

"But what about my news?"

I halted. "Tell me."

"The cats at Murphy's house are talking about doing in the old lady."

"Doing in Mrs. Murphy?"

"No, cupcake, doing in the Psi Phi house mother." He licked a paw delicately.

"How in the world are a bunch of cats going to do that?" I was impatient to leave.

"Don't you get it, girl? The cats are working for Barnaby. They're masterminding his coming-out party. Trying to catch the Protector unawares. Heard they're sending some vampires in the next blood van."

I knew the next blood drive was scheduled for later today. "These cats, how many are there?"

"I'd guess around a dozen, give or take."

"Thanks, er, what's your name?"

"Name's Fluffy. I was living with Murphy before those

Avarice Demons moved in. Now I'm prowling around, looking for a new gig. Thinking maybe you could set me up at the Psi Phi House."

"Dude, you are so barking up the wrong tree."

"Hey, I was good to you. Now it's your turn to be good to me." He stamped his paw in annoyance.

"If what you say is true, then I'll do what I can. But I can't make any promises."

He sniggered at me, the little poop. "Some all-powerful Slayer you are. Can't even find a home for a helpless cat."

"I said I'd try; give it a rest." And I ran the rest of the way to Psi Phi House.

I arrived in time to smell fresh cookies baking in the oven. It was marvelous. Aunt Chloe was orchestrating treats for the anticipated donors. The sullen faces of half-bloods had me realizing they were not helping out of the kindness of their hearts.

"Why the long faces?" I asked Angie.

"Would you want to be baking cookies you can't eat?"

She made an excellent point. "Where's Aunt Chloe?"

She tossed her wild brown hair in the direction of the kitchen. Aunt Chloe was issuing orders like a drill sergeant.

"Pick up the pace, ladies. If you want to get to bed, you have to finish this last batch. You can't get something for nothing, you know."

"I did last night." One of the new girls tittered and several others joined in.

"I'm not talking about that, girlie. I'm talking about blood. If you want to feed, you have to give back to the community. Those are the rules. How often you want to be listed on the ho chart is up to you."

The girl gasped, but kept quiet after that. You had to love Aunt Chloe.

"Have you seen Colby?" I asked as soon as I was noticed.

"No dear, she went to school early this morning. What's wrong?"

I debated telling her about the cat's message. I didn't feel like sounding crazy in front of the other inhabitants of the House, so I just shook my head and asked to use the phone.

After a quick call to Animal Control complaining about the poor health and living conditions of the cats at Mrs. Murphy's house, I tried to call Hunter again. This time a very groggy Slayer answered the phone.

"Yeah."

"Morning, sunshine. Everything okay over there?" I jumped to the point right away.

"Piper?" He was still muddled.

"Yeah it's Piper. Expecting another girl to call and wake you up?" I tried not to sound jealous, but really. I hardly knew anything about the guy except he was a Demon Slayer and too sexy for words.

"Sorry, I'm just so tired. Hard to wake up this morning. I need some tea." I smiled at his reference to tea instead of coffee. We always met at the teahouse.

"Anything unusual happen this morning? Any unexpected visitors?" I tried to keep the urgency out of my voice. After all, I only had the word of a very suspicious cat.

"No, I don't think so. 'Course I've been dead to the world so a football team could have played through here and I wouldn't have noticed."

Nice to know Demon Slayers were such light sleepers. Not.

"Great, well, meet me at the teahouse in an hour, okay?"

"Will do." And he hung up.

I should have known better than to believe that Colby was going after Demon Slayer blood. I was such a fool. That cat was gonna get it the next time it crossed my path. But still, I shouldn't take any chances so I flagged down Angie, who was heading the blood drive.

"Angie, I think maybe some demons might be after Aunt Chloe. I heard they might crash the blood drive. Can you have Tribunal Security greet the van?"

"Sure, but why not ask Thomas to do it?"

Yeah, that would work. Let me ask the guy being possessed by the head demon to protect us. Thomas had no idea what was happening and I couldn't be sure Barnaby couldn't read Thomas's thoughts.

"Have you seen Thomas?" I asked instead.

She shook her head. "No, but I can call security. No biggie."

I watched her pull a cell out of her jeans and flip it open. Great, that should help ward off any unsavory surprises.

Colby entered the house about a half hour later. I was

waiting for her in the living room. The cookie patrol had long since headed to bed.

"Hey," she said, slowing removing a hoodie when she saw me.

"Hi." We were both shy in light of our recent argument. "Where you been?"

She shook out her hair and it fell back into perfect form. Straight and sleek, blonde and beautiful.

"School, then breakfast. You're here early."

"Yeah, I got a line on some demon activity I thought you should know about."

Colby's face took on the same exasperated expression she wore the last time we spoke. I tapped down my irritation and decided to give her a quick heads-up then go meet Hunter.

"Don't. Just don't, okay. I know you don't believe me but you need to know that Barnaby is going after Aunt Chloe to distract you. It's going to happen at the blood drive. Zombie vamps in the van."

"I would ask how you came by this information but let me guess: talking cat, right?"

I stopped in front of her. "You know, you make it very hard to like you sometimes."

She rewarded me with a long-suffering sigh. "Look, I know how hard it is for you. I really do. You think I signed up for this? Being the Protector's best friend probably sucks almost as much as being the Protector does. But it is what it is. It doesn't mean you're not important or special. You mean the world to me. You don't have to be a Demon Slayer for me to respect you."

Have you ever met a cheerleader who didn't have an ego? Make her Undead and give her a purpose like protecting half-bloods and I'll show a very self-centered vampire.

I took her by the shoulders and said slowly, "I know this is hard for you, but just try to focus. My being a Demon Slayer has nothing to do with you being the Protector. It has nothing to do with you, *period*. Difficult though that is for you to grasp, do us both a favor and just try, okay?"

I was done trying to convince her. I was going to help her, whether she wanted it or not, because that was my job.

She touched my shoulder and said, "It's not that I don't believe you Piper. It's just—"

"You want proof? Well, I can't give you that unless you have a possessed cat around I can talk to; but then, you wouldn't know it was talking back to me, would you? You would have to take my word on it. And we know how good you are at that nowadays."

"Piper, that's not fair!"

"You know you aren't perfect, right? I think maybe you're a little confused about that. People need help once in a while. You're not an island unto yourself, Colby. It doesn't make you weak or bad at your job if you ask for help."

She took a step back. "You can't help me, Piper."

"Just watch out for Aunt Chloe, you egomaniac." I

slammed the door on my way out, hard. She was the most exasperating person sometimes. I must have had the patience of a saint not to write her off and go home. But unlike Colby, I could recognize when a situation wasn't all about me.

It was time to meet Hunter.

Thirteen

COLBY

Call me an egomaniac, would she? Hah! If she was *really* a Demon Slayer, then Ms. Weatherbee would have sent me to get *her* blood and not that of a real Demon Slayer, that bad boy from the mall that found us in the parking garage. He was trouble, exactly like I said to Piper. Why didn't she listen to me? She had to be right all the time. It was exasperating.

I managed to get the blood I needed and a little breakfast without him so much as waking up. Some Demon Slayer. If I'd been Barnaby, the only thing left of him would be a scuffed pair of boots.

I wisely kept the details of my morning from Piper. I didn't need her getting all over me for that too. I'm sure she would have jumped to his defense and said he could help us if we just trusted him. Yeah, trust a Demon Slayer not to kill Thomas if he suspected him of being possessed? Not likely.

As for Piper being a Demon Slayer, I refused to even dwell on it. That would mean she would try to kill Thomas and that was ludicrous. Piper was not a cold-blooded killer.

The only time she'd ever killed was trying to save me in the parking garage. I couldn't even count the first time because I'd used her to trip the vampire. That was what staked him on the picket fence, not some glorious attack by my wussy best friend.

I found Aunt Chloe in the back of the house, getting ready to take a nap.

"Did you see Piper, my dear?" she asked when I peeked in her bedroom.

"Yeah, she's on her way out." I decided to sit on the bed and visit with her. It seemed we rarely saw each other, even though we lived in the same place.

"Hmm, probably meeting that boy on the motorcycle. Not that I blame her. I wouldn't mind meeting him." She winked at me.

I became very still. "What boy?"

She pulled the covers down and said, "That one you two were fighting over. The one from the garage. They went out the other night. He took her to a cemetery, isn't that something? Very original. Didn't she tell you?"

I stood up. "No, she didn't mention it."

"Probably thought you'd disapprove. You need to have more faith in your friends, my dear."

I walked woodenly toward the door. Stopping, I looked

back at her. "Aunt Chloe, I want to be the one to greet the blood van this afternoon, okay? I think I should be more involved in House activities."

She looked confused but nodded in agreement. "If you want, dear. Van arrives at four."

It was silly of me, but I wasn't going to risk Aunt Chloe's life. And anyway, no vampire zombie would be hiding in a van that we would open during the day, with the sun out. Of course, a possessed vampire wouldn't be so concerned about burning to death in the sunlight if it thought it could jump into another body right away. A body like Aunt Chloe's.

No, it was hardly plausible, but I would meet the van regardless. I should be more visible around the House anyway. We had new members who really didn't know me. It would be good for everyone.

Putting my vial of blood on the desk, I changed clothes and slept until early afternoon. I woke up sneezing and heard a crash followed by a yowl. WTF?

In the far corner of my room was an orange cat, hissing, teeth bared and backed into a corner. On the floor was the vial of blood, shattered, crushed beneath my computer speaker.

"Sophie!" I bellowed, ready to kill the maid. Momentarily, Ileana and Sophie entered my room, looking very confused. The cat slashed out with its claws and snarled.

"You brought another cat into the house," I accused. "And it wrecked my room."

Sophie looked around for damage. "But I didn't, miss.

Not since you said I could have another pet. I swear it." She appeared frightened, wringing her hands.

As soon as she said it, I knew it was true. Sophie was the worst liar on the planet. She wore every emotion on her face. She really had no idea about the cat.

But I was still mad. "Who let it in here, then?"

The cat sensed its chance for a quick getaway and flew past them, out the door. I wanted to chase it but Ileana said, "Let it go. It's too late. The damage is done."

I had to agree. The damage was done. My Slayer blood was smeared all over the hardwood, kitty paws effectively spreading it out so there was no way I could save any of it.

I dropped down on the bed, numb. "What am I going to do?"

Neither had an answer for me but I knew. I had to get more. I had to find Hunter. Throwing on my clothes, I barked, "Make sure that cat is out of the house."

Within minutes I was rushing to the teahouse where I thought I'd find Piper. The gal behind the counter said she was there earlier, but left with a smokin' hot guy on a motorcycle. This did *not* thrill me.

I called her cell and each time it went directly to voice mail. Dead battery or she had turned it off. Checking my watch, I discovered it was quarter to four. In my excitement, I almost forgot about meeting the blood van.

It was weird, walking back to Psi Phi House. It seemed everywhere I looked, a cat was watching me. I swore I saw the same orange cat that sabotaged my potion and numerous others. At least five of them. If Piper hadn't told me demons possessed cats I never would have noticed them but somehow, each one had a sinister quality.

I made it home in less than ten minutes. Inside the house, several sun-friendly half-bloods were putting out cookies and orange juice in anticipation of students donating blood. I tried Piper's cell again and almost threw my phone against the wall in frustration when voice mail picked up immediately. Time was running out, I was sure of it.

It would happen soon and I wasn't ready. Not near ready. I helped out and paced the floor. I greeted donors, asking them to make themselves at home. Aunt Chloe kept checking the time and making *tsk*ing sounds. At four thirty she called her friend at the blood bank. Yes, the van had left over an hour ago and no, they hadn't heard from them.

It was official. The van was late. After fifteen more minutes, Aunt Chloe's friend called back to say they couldn't raise the driver on his cell phone. I had a very bad feeling in the pit of my stomach.

I left the house and was surprised to see some Tribunal Security standing guard outside the house.

"What are you guys doing here?"

Angie saw me and intercepted. "I called them. Piper thought there would be some trouble with the blood van and asked me to have security here. I guess if you can call not showing up trouble, then she was right."

I nodded in agreement. That was very high-handed of Piper—and extremely thoughtful, I had to grudgingly admit. Where was she? Time was running out. I had to mix the potion soon and I still needed Slayer blood.

At seven o'clock I was ready to admit defeat. Not a word from Piper or Thomas. No blood van and a bunch of hungry, cranky half-bloods complaining how they worked so hard to make cookies and now they couldn't even enjoy those.

I left the House to meet Ms. Weatherbee. I would have to make the potion without the blood. It was that simple. I was out of time and options. Whatever was going to happen was going to happen tonight. I knew it.

I arrived just as Ms. Weatherbee did.

"Are you ready to boil and brew?"

I got straight to the point. "I don't have the Slayer blood."

"You couldn't get it?" She seemed surprised.

"Oh no, I got it. Then a cat smashed it."

"What do you want to do? Do you want to wait?"

"I don't think we can wait. I think something is going to happen soon. Like tonight soon."

She nodded in agreement. "I agree. The signs are everywhere."

I ignored her mystic prediction. "Let's make the potion without the blood."

"But, Colby—"

"I understand the risks, it can't be helped. Let's just make it up."

She nodded and we gathered all the ingredients and headed to an unoccupied lab. She fired up a Bunsen burner then started adding ingredients. Mixing, pouring, crushing, reducing. The process took hours.

"You know, you may still be in luck. The blood doesn't need to cook with the potion. It just needs to be added after these ingredients stew. If you get some, you can still use it."

"You're very much an optimist, aren't you, Ms. Weatherbee?" I couldn't help but comment. Sadly, I couldn't share her sunny outlook.

"I believe you will do what's right when the moment arrives."

"You wouldn't happen to know what that is, would you?"

She put the last of the potion in a glass vial and stopped it with a black cork. She smiled as she gave it to me.

"You gotta have faith."

I nodded, taking the formula. It was still warm from the burner, but not so hot I couldn't hold it.

"Do you have the other things you need?"

I made a face. "Yes, in my backpack."

"Then good luck." She caught me by surprise when she reached out to hug me.

"Thank you." I nodded and left her in the lab. I had my potion, minus one crucial ingredient.

I left campus and made a beeline to Psi Phi House. No one called me on my cell to say the blood van finally arrived and

Piper hadn't returned my many calls. I was not pleased. I was even more annoyed when a black cat popped out from the bushes and meowed at me.

I felt like kicking it but could hardly bring myself to harm a helpless cat that just happened to be in my path. This one didn't emit a sinister vibe.

"Not in the mood, cat," I said as it meowed again, sounding as pathetic as any cat could.

"I don't have any food for you, so beat it." The cat rushed toward me, stopped, turned around several times and meowed again.

"Okay, you've got my attention. Now what do you want?"

I stopped and waited for it to react. It sat back on its bottom and pawed the air, like it was trying to play with dangling string. Oh brother, I so don't have time for this.

I started walking again and the cat raced toward me and took a swipe at my ankle. "Ouch!" I grabbed at my leg.

It sat back down and shook its paws frantically. It wasn't playing, as I originally thought. It was pointing between two houses. Then it jumped up and walked in that direction, looking over its shoulder at me, as though expecting me to follow.

"I've got to be crazy," I muttered, deciding to go. It seemed pleased that I finally understood what it wanted and rushed ahead. It weaved behind houses, through an alley and crept slowly toward an older Tudor house whose lawn looked in desperate need of a mow.

It was Mrs. Murphy's house. The cat lady.

We cautiously made our way toward the side of the house, where the unattached garage was located. A screen of high, overgrown hedges obscured the neighbors from view. The cat dove into the greenery. Oh, I was so not going into the bushes.

"Psst, Colby," I heard a voice from the hedge. Was the cat talking to me?

"Psst! Colby, over here." This time I recognized the whisper. It was Piper.

I crept closer and scurried under branches to a small denlike haven within the bushes. Piper was there, leaves in her hair and the black cat by her side.

"Your new apartment is a little small for my taste," I commented dryly, trying to position myself in the tight quarters.

"Yeah, but it's got a great view." She pulled the lowest branch to the side so we had an unobstructed view of the garage and side door of the house.

"And this would interest you, why?"

The cat meowed and Piper nodded in agreement. "You have no idea," she said to it.

"You wanna tell me what's going on?"

"Demons in the house. Hunter's in the blood van in the garage."

"The blood van's in the garage?" I took a peek over her shoulder.

"Yeah, they had a little glitch in their plan." The cat meowed again and Piper smiled. "They so did not see that one coming, huh?"

"Are you talking to the cat?"

"No, I'm talking to the Sloth Demon inside the cat." Her shoulders stiffened. "But then I don't expect you to believe that."

I ignored her last comment and asked instead, "What glitch?"

"I called the Humane Society on them. They took away about ten possessed cats this afternoon. It was great." The cat meowed in agreement.

"Hunter and I decided to head off the blood van but things got a little messy and he was captured. I couldn't leave in case they tried to move him or hurt him so I sent Mr. Whiskers to find you. Took him long enough." The cat starting meowing in self-defense to which Piper responded, "Yeah, yeah, tell it to the judge."

"Mr. Whiskers?" I echoed.

"He used to live at Mrs. Murphy's until all the Avarice Demons started possessing the regular cats. They've possessed Mrs. Murphy now, too."

As if on cue, the house door swung open and we crouched farther back in the shadows. Mrs. Murphy and two zombie vampires walked over to the garage and entered. Mr. Whiskers immediately jumped up and followed them. He loitered just outside the open garage.

"Can you hear anything?" Piper asked me. I strained my

head in the direction of the conversation but couldn't make anything out. All the voices sounded like they were buzzing with electrical interference.

"No." We waited in uncomfortable silence. Finally, I said, "You know it's not that I don't want you to be a Demon Slayer. Well, no, that's not true. I don't want you to be one, but not for the reasons you think."

She glanced in my direction so I continued. "It's just since I became Undead and had this whole Protector thing dumped in my lap, I'm always in danger and have this constant pressure on me to save the world. It's overwhelming and I look at you and your life—" My voice broke so I cleared my throat. "I just look at your life and I'm so envious. I wish I could be you so badly that I want to keep you safe and normal and sort of live my life through you."

She shifted her weight and looked at me with confusion.

"Don't you see if you're a Demon Slayer then you have all the same crap to deal with that I do without the benefit of being immortal? You could die, Piper. Way easier than I can."

"Is that why you've been such a jerk about accepting my being a Demon Slayer? You know, putting your head in the sand and denying it is not going to make it any less true," she pointed out.

"I know, but it's just so . . ." I struggled to make sense. "So hard. Sometimes I just can't deal with it all."

She put her hand on my shoulder. "I know, Colby. I get it. I don't know how you do it all. I'm scared to death about be-

ing a Demon Slayer. You know how I am! Hunter got captured and did I save him? No, I'm hiding in the bushes waiting for you to come and save my butt. Like always," she
ended bitterly.

"There is a huge difference between being a coward and
playing the odds. You are the bravest person I know, Piper.
There's no one I would rather have my back."

"Really? Even Thomas?"

"Right now? Especially Thomas." I gave her a wry smile.

"You'll save Thomas," she assured me.

"No, we'll save Thomas. And Hunter too."

Just then the cat came back, and Mrs. Murphy left the
garage to return to the house.

Piper listened to the cat, seemingly impatient with its explanation.

"What? What is it?"

"The demons are standing guard over Hunter. They're
moving him into the house." A crack of thunder reverberated
through the air, catching us both by surprise. Lightening
flashed.

"They're going to open the portal between the worlds to
let Barnaby come through with a legion of followers."

"Where will the legion go? It's not like there's a bunch of
cats or vampires hanging around."

The cat meowed again. "The storm. They'll live in the
charged particles until their hosts arrive."

"What hosts?" I wanted to know.

"I don't know. It looks like I messed with the plan by calling the Humane Society. We've got to save Hunter."

She made a move to leave the bushes but I stopped her. "No way we're going to bust into that garage without any weapons. We have no idea what's in store for us in there. Sounds like they want him alive so he isn't in any immediate danger. Anyway, I have an idea how to get Barnaby, but I need some time."

"You want me just to sit and wait in the shadows and do nothing? I don't think so."

"No, I want you to get captured by the demons after you're properly armed, but first I want some blood."

Her eyes got big. "Are you kidding me? You're hungry at a time like this?"

I smacked her shoulder. "No, you idiot. I need the blood of a Demon Slayer for my potion and last time I checked, you were the only Demon Slayer around, so it's time to bleed a little for me."

"You believe me?"

"Of course I believe you. I'm staking our lives on it—hand over a vein." She offered her left arm to me. I took out my fang headgear and gave her one last chance to back down.

I gave her the potion beaker to hold under the wound and nodded that I was ready. She took a deep breath and nodded back. I put her wrist up to my mouth and licked it, numbing the area. She shivered but kept her arm still. I knew how difficult this must be for her and I was so proud.

Slowly, I pierced the skin, fighting the desire to swallow her life essence and instead pulled away, watching the blood start to pool and drip into the potion. Piper looked positively green and I worried she was going to faint but her breathing stayed low and even. The cat meowed and she shook her head no. It moved closer and rubbed its head against her leg in a show of support. I tried not to sneeze.

When I had enough, or at least hoped I had enough, I licked the wound and it healed instantly. She pulled back, checking her wrist for scars.

"My turn." I bit my own wrist and dropped a few drops in as well. We didn't need much of my blood, so I licked the wound and took off my headgear.

"What is this stuff anyway?" she asked, swirling it in the vial so the blood mixed with the shimmering black liquid.

"It's our secret weapon."

"Really?" She looked doubtful.

Before I could explain, a car arrived. We peeked past the branches to get a better look. Two more zombie vampires arrived. They were escorting—oh no, it was Thomas! He looked dazed and exhausted. They pushed him forward. I noticed his hands were bound. So, Barnaby hadn't fully possessed him yet. I was relieved.

The atmosphere crackled and the sky took on a reddish

glow. Lightning continued to strike, accompanied by thunderous booms. We were running out of time.

I pulled a few things out of my bag that caused Piper's eyes to widen. "You have got to be joking me," she said when I laid them out on the ground. The cat made a sound like it agreed.

"I can't do it myself, I don't have a mirror." I took out a piece of paper from my pants, unfolded it and laid it next to the implements.

"Do me first and then it's your turn."

"What?" she squawked.

"You can't go in there unprotected. Period. It's either this or you go back to Psi Phi House."

We had a stare-down but she finally relented. "Oh fine. But this totally sucks, you know that, right?"

"How's it feel to be a Demon Slayer now, huh?"

She pointedly ignored me and began the task.

Fourteen

PIPER

My chest hurt. I purposely crept too close to the house and made a ton of unnecessary noise to be heard above the storm. I tripped over a hose I couldn't see in the long grass and fell into the porch fence. I'd have bruises, I was sure. Mrs. Murphy herself came out to see what the ruckus was and grabbed my arm with incredible strength.

They needed hosts for the demon invasion and I played right into her hand. That was why they were keeping Hunter alive as well. We couldn't be possessed if we were already dead. Timing was everything. Comforting thought, that.

She dragged me inside and threw me next to Hunter. He looked awful. Either he put up a big fight or they just beat the crap out of him for fun, I couldn't be sure. I tried to wipe away the blood on his face with my sleeve. He moaned.

"Run," he tried to say. "Run."

"Shh, be still." I continued to minister to his face. "Everything's going to be okay. I promise."

His hands were tied behind him so I helped prop him up so he was more comfortable. One of the zombies made a threatening gesture at me.

"Oh, relax. We'll be zombies soon enough. Don't you want one of your little friends to inhabit a comfortable, strong body instead of an invalid?"

The zombie was confused and looked to Mrs. Murphy for guidance. Yep, she was definitely in charge around here.

"Leave them. There's nothing they can do now."

She walked toward Thomas, who was seated at the dining room table, head slumped to his chest. I'd never seen him look worse.

She caressed his cheek lovingly, running an aged, withered hand across his chest. Ohmigod! Colby was going to freak when she saw this. It looked like Barnaby had a girlfriend in Mrs. Murphy.

I pretended to help Hunter sit up but really dropped a blade from inside my sleeve down to my hand and ran it across the duct tape holding him captive. Hunter stirred in surprise. It would take several passes to get his hands free so I pressed the blade into his hand and pretended to cower in fear next to him, putting my hands in plain view so the zombie who was guarding us wouldn't get suspicious.

"What's the plan?" he asked between swollen lips.

"We're Plan B. Don't worry," I assured him.

"Piper—"

"Shhhh. Trust me."

He fell silent, working industriously on freeing his hands.

Colby arrived, making an entrance the zombies weren't likely to forget. She kicked the door down and stood at the threshold demanding, "Barnaby!"

Two zombies rushed her but she easily tossed them out of her way. Mrs. Murphy approached, yielding a wicked-looking sword.

"Cool it, grandma," Colby said. "I'm not here to rain on your parade. I'm here to talk to Barnaby. He offered me a very interesting deal the last time we met."

Mrs. Murphy faltered, looking back toward Thomas. Thunder crashed and the room exploded with light from the storm brewing outside. It had been going on for hours and hours. I imagined thousands of demons whirling around in the air, waiting to possess their hosts and become the army Barnaby wanted.

Hunter's eyes widened. He finally knew who the Protector was and I could see his shock. Colby Blanchard looked more like a high school cheerleader than an Undead Protector. Mrs. Murphy seemed to share his disbelief.

"You're the Protector?" she said in synthesized shock.

"Never judge a book by its cover, grandma. I'm sure you're stronger than you look."

Colby glanced around the room; her eyes rested on me for a moment. It was a warning. Murphy would be tough. I nodded.

Suddenly Thomas stirred, his eyes aglow with demonic strength. His face was drawn and haggard but I gave an involuntary gasp. He did look possessed. What would Colby do?

"As you can see, I'm unarmed." She raised her hands in mock surrender. She was wearing jeans and a pink Psi Phi House hoodie.

When Murphy didn't move, Thomas stirred in his chair. "I knew you would come. It was written all those years ago that you would rule by my side. Come to me, Colby."

She cocked her head to one side. "What's up with the handcuffs, Barnaby? I'm not into the kinky stuff."

"Merely a precaution, my sweet. My full possession is not complete. I wouldn't want any surprises from your Thomas. His defeat is imminent but still he struggles."

"You mean this isn't a done deal yet? Do you have any idea what would happen to me if you don't keep up your end of the bargain?"

Hunter stirred next to me, struggling to free his hands and attack her. I held him back. Please, she was so overacting. Couldn't he see that? Men were so blinded by what they wanted to see they couldn't look objectively past their own prejudices.

Colby took a step closer to Thomas but Murphy pointed the sword at her. "Come no closer. I protect my master."

Colby stopped and put her hands on her hips. "I will not be playing second fiddle to Haggy McHag over here, Barnaby."

Murphy advanced on Colby, hissing; Thomas's laughter filled the room. "My pet, how splendid you are. Bring her to me."

Murphy reluctantly lowered her weapon, and stepped aside so Colby could join Thomas. Hunter finally freed himself but I shook my head. It wasn't time. I'd promised Colby not to interfere unless her play failed. She hadn't made her move, so for now, we watched and waited.

"Let's make our move," Hunter whispered.

"No, we're Plan B," I stubbornly insisted.

"Are you crazy? She's already in league with him. They'll end us all if we don't act." He tried to move but I elbowed him in the ribs.

"No!" I hissed quietly. "You have to trust me. If you care for me at all, Hunter, you'll do this for me. Just let it play out."

His struggle was visible. He wanted to believe me but was scared to let go of his preconceived notions and have faith in Colby and myself.

Finally, he nodded curtly and watched Colby play the role of evil villainess.

She marched right up to Barnaby, as I could see no sign of Thomas left. I prayed we weren't too late. "Let me free you, my lord," Colby purred, placing her hand on his cheek in a caress. "Nothing can stop us now that we are together."

Barnaby's reaction was swift. Being incorporeal for so long, now that he could feel emotion the touch of another person made him greedy for her.

He grabbed the front of her sweatshirt with his captive hands and viciously kissed her. She didn't struggle, but pulled him closer, ripping his shirt open, exposing his chest while opening herself to his assault. When they finally parted, her mouth was bleeding and his fangs were out.

I clutched Hunter's arm, unaware of how my fingernails were digging into his flesh until he flexed his muscles. I immediately relaxed my grip. Colby had to kiss that gross demon, full on the mouth, tongue and everything. I wanted to puke but imagined Colby wanted to more.

He demanded, "Remove my bonds."

"But, Master, it's too soon," Mrs. Murphy argued, though she advanced to do his bidding.

Colby whipped forward, grabbing the keys out of the hag's hands. "He's all-powerful. A god. He must be freed."

She turned back to him, a seductive smile on her face, which must've hurt because her lower lip was cut. He held out his hands when a tremor shook him. For a moment, I could actually see Thomas emerge. "Kill me, Colby. Kill me before it's too late!" he cried.

She laughed in a really ruthless, hurtful way. "Now why would I do that? Go away, Thomas. It's time for the big kids to play."

At her urging, Thomas seemed to give up and leave. Barnaby reemerged, laughing cruelly. "We shall rule the world together."

Colby nimbly unlocked his cuffs, throwing them playfully behind her. He reached for her face, and kissed her again, this time less brutally. I noted how her hands stayed in front of her chest and held my breath. She was making her move. I slid a wooden stake out of the other sleeve of my sweatshirt, gripping it tightly. Hunter had the blade and I had a stake. That was I all I could smuggle in. Murphy had a sword and I knew she would be the one we had to take out before she could get to Colby.

"We have to take out Murphy before she can get to Colby," I whispered, surprising Hunter. "Wait for the signal."

"What is the signal?" he asked, but just then it came and there was no mistaking it.

Colby unzipped her hoodie while Barnaby kissed her and pulled it wide, then flung her arms around him and held him tightly to her. An unearthly scream filled the air. For a moment, Murphy stood transfixed. What was going on? Then she saw the smoke rise from between their bodies, and the smell of cooking flesh filled the air. Hunter was ready to pounce; he dove at Murphy while I took on the closest zombie vamp.

I was terrified but didn't freeze. It was an amazing thing actually, the way my body sort of took over and my mind calculated the distance to stake the vamp. In two steps, I drove the wood into his heart and *poof*, the mist escaped as he collapsed.

Turning to the next foe, which was about to stab Hunter from behind, I kicked him in the back of the knee, dropping him instantly.

Hunter barely noticed, so intent on getting to Murphy before she got to Colby. Barnaby screamed and screamed, trying to pull away from her, but Colby held tight. I knew she could use Barnaby as a shield if Murphy got close enough but she wouldn't do that. Barnaby was in Thomas's body and she would never harm Thomas. She would die first.

I was so proud of Hunter. He dodged Murphy's sword, small blade in hand, and when she made her play to stab Colby, he effectively blocked it with a blow to the eye. Yuck! A hiss of mist escaped and he quickly took her sword and lopped off her head. Gross!

It had to be done—Mrs. Murphy wasn't a vampire, she was human. She wasn't decaying and he needed to make sure nothing could try to inhabit her body. I was glad he had that duty to perform, not me. He quickly did the same to the zombie whose knee I took out.

I rushed to Colby, who still held Barnaby, but his screams seemed to have stopped. She was crying, and when she finally released Thomas, his body crumbled to the ground. Were we too late?

Fifteen

COLBY

I couldn't seem to stop crying. And not because my chest hurt from the brand or from the disgusting lip-lock with a demon, but because Thomas wasn't moving. I was too late. Hunter rushed up, still holding a sword, but all I could think about was how Thomas wasn't moving. If the Demon Slayer decided to kill me, I'm not sure I could have fought him. I felt empty inside.

"Colby, are you okay?" Piper was pulling my hoodie open to see the damage the tattoo caused.

When we sat together, huddled in the bushes, giving each other homemade tattoos using the special potion Ms. Weatherbee brewed for me, I didn't think it would hurt so much. Sure, the razor-sharp needles bundled together and poked continuously into my chest was far from a good time, but the burning sensation continued long after the needles left my body. That was the real killer.

It was the liquid silver that kept me from healing the tattoo immediately. It bubbled and erupted like an ugly black brand. On Piper, it had a different effect. It gave her tattoo a shimmery quality.

The plan was that the symbol on me, pressed against Thomas's chest, would brand him. Effectively protecting him against demon possession and sealing our souls together by replacing the missing piece of his essence with my own. Entwined with each other for all eternity. Without Thomas, I would never be whole again and without me, neither would he.

"It isn't working. Thomas is gone." I moaned, ignoring Piper's attempt to inspect my brand.

I was wearing only a bra under the zip-up hoodie. She tattooed the symbol directly over my heart, so that when I pulled open my sweatshirt, the brand would connect directly with his skin. Hence the need to rip off his shirt while kissing him. I couldn't imagine how it looked to Hunter, who was convinced I would bring forth the end of the world. Seeing me lip-lock a demon would certainly make a convincing argument that I was evil.

"How are they?" Hunter wanted to know, rushing tenderly to Piper's side. I noted how he touched her hair in concern. He loved her. He might not know it yet, but he did. Piper was too wrapped up in my wound to notice.

I pulled away, directing my attention to the man I loved. "Get up, Thomas," I begged softly. "You've got to get up." I became increasingly more agitated when his body remained lifeless.

I got right into his face and screamed, "Dammit, Thomas, get up! Do you have any idea what I had to do in order to save you? I had to kiss a demon. Twice. Now I have this big, ugly tattoo on my chest." I yanked on his shoulders, shaking him.

"Get up. Get up. Get up!" I demanded, over and over again. I was unaware of the room filling with Tribunal Security until Mr. Holloway laid a hand on my shoulder.

"It's over, Colby," he said sadly. It was the way he said it, with such finality, that broke something inside of me. No, it wasn't over. It wasn't over until I said it was over. I reached back and slapped Thomas, hard. His head snapped to one side and I heard Piper gasp.

"Get up!" I screamed and slapped him again. Mr. Holloway tried to restrain me but I slapped once more. This time, it was Thomas's hand that stopped the blow.

"It's bad enough you were kissing a demon, do you have to beat me senseless too?" he whispered through cracked lips.

Piper squealed. I pulled him into my arms and kissed his face all over. He was okay. He was alive. Well, he wasn't technically alive but he was back and that was all I wanted.

I helped him into a sitting position and checked out the tattoo on his chest. It was a big, ugly brand that matched mine. Blech, we would no longer be attending any pool parties, that's for sure.

"Anyone want to tell me why I'm sitting in the middle of a house that smells like cats?" he asked weakly.

I gave Piper a look. Where did we start?

"You were slowly being possessed by an Avarice Demon named Barnaby," I began. Piper nodded in agreement.

"How did you know that?" He was incredulous.

"You had bad dreams, couldn't sleep and were irritable. You did irrational things like send Carl away to New York and one time, Barnaby actually possessed you in your sleep and talked to me. That was kind of the clincher."

He nodded. "Yeah, that would do it. You saved me?"

"Of course. It was really the new library exhibit that gave me the idea how."

"What library exhibit?" he asked. Mr. Holloway looked bewildered as well.

"The one you brought back to the library, Thomas—you don't remember that?"

Thomas shook his head. "I don't really remember much of anything. I suspected I was having bad dreams but I think I've been blacking out as well. I'd remember going to bed but I'd wake up in strange places. Places I didn't remember going to. I wondered if I was going crazy.

"I do remember a fire of some sort. In catacombs filled with books. It's like I was watching someone else. I—I don't really remember the details."

Hunter seemed to be agitated and backed away from us. Piper followed but I was more concerned with Thomas.

"When it was obvious you were being possessed, I did some research and discovered that Demon Slayers used a symbol to protect their body from being possessed if they died. I found the ingredients for the tattoo ink and made some up. Then Piper helped me tattoo it on my chest. I had to wait until Barnaby was in our world before I could put the symbol on you. That way you would be protected and he couldn't escape back to his own world to try again later."

"Where is he now?" Thomas wanted to know.

"Up there, with his followers." I nodded toward the electrical activity in the sky, which was abating. "Once the storm is gone, they won't be able to survive here. The only thing keeping them going is the electricity."

"We should get you to Psi Phi House, Thomas," Mr. Holloway stated. "You did a fine job, Colby, I knew I could count on you."

Praise. Who doesn't love it? "Thank you, sir, but I couldn't have done it without Piper. Where did she go, anyway?" I looked around for her but she and Hunter were gone.

Thomas groaned while I helped him up. He clutched his chest. "This thing hurts. Even more than demon possession."

I decided the explanation about soul mates should wait until we got him back to the House. I knew about Hunter's family and the fire. Piper had told me when we were doing the tattoo thing.

I hoped Hunter realized that it wasn't Thomas who'd done that terrible thing, but Barnaby. He probably needed some time to think. I was glad Piper went with him.

*   *   *

We arrived at Psi Phi House to the usual bustle of activity. No one had suspected Thomas was being possessed by a demon—except Ileana, of course. The girls had no idea they were almost destroyed in a demon invasion, which was as it should be. My job as Protector was to keep them from danger.

Although they'd hear about it eventually. Mr. Holloway was having a bulletin sent to all vampires about the situation. We needed to be vigilant to keep this from happening again.

"So it worked," Ileana murmured in approval while I was getting Thomas a warm washcloth.

"Yeah, and check out this ugly brand." I unzipped my sweatshirt and showed her.

She nodded. "Does he know what the brand means, other than demon protection?"

"No, I'm not sure how to bring that up. I mean, what do I say? 'Hey, honey, when you were possessed by a demon, I fused our souls together and now we're entwined for all eternity. Hope you don't mind'?" I shook my head. "It's totally insane."

"Now he will never again have to worry about being possessed by a demon. That is a great fear for full-bloods. I'm sure he'll be grateful for that. As for being entwined with *you* for eternity, well, that's another matter."

"Nice. Remind me never to choose you to write a toast in my honor."

She smirked and wandered back toward the living room, where Thomas was relaxing on one of the fluffy couches.

I returned with washcloth in hand and gently washed his neck and face. At first, he put up a fight about all the fussing but it didn't take long for him to enjoy the extra attention. I waited until we were finally alone before I broached the subject.

"Thomas, how worried were you about demon possession before this happened?"

He thought a long moment. "It's a concern most older vampires have. The ones who have been around a long while. They tend to get paranoid and that's part of the process. I honestly didn't worry about it until I started having those crazy dreams. By then, I guess it was too late. I wasn't in full control and I couldn't remember large blocks of time."

"The symbol on your chest will protect you from demon possession but it has an extra, let's call it, feature as well," I told him.

He looked puzzled. "Really? What's that?"

"I sort of fixed your whole missing piece of essence problem."

"What do you mean?"

"You see, vampires can't really get tattoos. We heal so quickly that a traditional tattoo disappears right away. We sort of stay the way we looked when we became Undead."

He nodded impatiently. Every vampire knew that.

I struggled with a tactful way to put the next part. I felt like I was about to confess a shotgun wedding. "The only way for my plan to work was to create a potion that lasted on the Undead. It required the help of a witch, er, a Magick Engineer."

His furrowed brow was a great indication that he was still clueless as to where I was taking this.

"So, the potion doesn't just make a permanent tattoo. It's a spell that filled the empty hole of your soul with mine and kind of fused them so we are sort of one. Entwined. Soul mates."

I waited for the full implication of what I was saying to register with him. Did he realize that we were, in essence, married forever? If we separated or left each other, we would be incomplete.

He looked at me carefully. "And you were aware of this when you created the plan?"

"Yes."

"How did you feel about it?" His voice was carefully neutral.

"I was fine with it. I mean, I didn't really think it mattered since we were, you know, in love, but it occurred to me that you might not want to be saddled with me through eternity. I mean, you love me but that doesn't mean you want my soul replacing your missing essence." I was wringing the washcloth in my hands.

"Colby, you saved my life. And this isn't the first time. The minute I met you, I knew you were the one. Every vampire dreams of finding someone they can love; the fact that you were already Undead, that I wouldn't lose you to aging, was more than I could hope for." He sat up, swung his legs off the couch and took the washcloth from me.

"I knew the first time we met that my soul belonged to you." He took my hands in his. "We belong to each other, Colby. I'm yours forever and it seems you're stuck with me forever as well."

I smiled at his joke. "You're not mad?" I whispered.

"Are you?" he countered. I was shocked.

"How could I be mad? You would have done it for me. You wouldn't even have hesitated. I love you."

"So there was hesitation?" he teased.

I rolled my eyes. "Uh, yeah. Did you not see my new ugly tattoo? But I did it for you. Now that's true love, baby."

Sixteen

PIPER

"Hunter, please wait up. I know you're upset but can't you see it wasn't Thomas but Barnaby?" I tried to chase him down as he hurried out of the house.

I caught up to him and we walked down the street, away from Mrs. Murphy's house. We came to the park outside the University and Hunter sat at the first bench he came to. I joined him.

"I had to leave," he whispered when I didn't say anything more to him.

"I understand."

"No, I don't think you do." He shook his head. "I had to leave, not because Barnaby torched the archive," he said, looking into my eyes. "And I do recognize it wasn't Thomas but Barnaby."

I was relieved.

"I should have been there. I should have saved my grandfather. I quit being a Demon Slayer because I didn't like that it was forced upon me and now what? I'm still a Demon Slayer. I'll always be a Demon Slayer. But now I'm alone."

I thought about what he said. True, his family was gone, but he wasn't alone. He wasn't the last Demon Slayer. I was here. Maybe I wasn't born to it and raised with it, but I was a Demon Slayer nonetheless. I reached over and put my hand in his.

Mr. Whiskers found us sitting in contemplative silence.

"Word on the street is you took out Barnaby." He sat down in front of us.

"Not now, Mr. Whiskers," I said.

He ignored me. "And my buddy who used to live at Mrs. Murphy's has a new pad courtesy of the Huntress here." I'd forgotten about the gray cat that warned me about the plot to attack Aunt Chloe using the blood van.

"You know, it was pretty smart of you to call the animal police. They rounded up all those demons and really put a kink in Barnaby's plans. You saved the day, girlie. Thanks to my friend. You won't be forgettin' a promise, now will you?"

"I never promised. I said I'd see what I do."

The cat snorted. "A promise is a promise."

"Look, can't this wait? We're kind of in the middle of something." I looked meaningfully at Hunter.

The cat licked its right paw. "Sorry to hear about the family, Hunter, I liked your granddad. He was a great ol' Slayer. I missed him after he quit."

"He didn't quit, he retired," Hunter corrected.

The cat snorted again. "Hardly. A Slayer doesn't retire. Ever. You should know that. He quit. Plain and simple. He thought he could play with his books and study the journals but that's not what a Slayer does. He let Barnaby get the drop on him. Wouldn't fight him. Said he wasn't a Slayer anymore." The cat shook his head. "I've seen a fair amount of Slayers in my day but one thing is constant through them all. You can't quit who you are. To do anything else is suicide."

The cat stretched. "Now I'm counting on you to keep your word, missy. I'm sending my friend over to that fancy vampire house. You best make it right." And he left us in the park.

We were both stunned. How was Hunter going to take this news?

"It doesn't change anything," he said quietly. "I still could have protected him if I'd been there."

"Or you could have died with him," I stated the obvious. "Listen, you saved all of us tonight. We couldn't have done it without you. If Mrs. Murphy had gotten to Colby, it would have been all over. I'm very sorry about what happened to your grandfather, I really am; but you have a gift and, as much as you hate it, you have a responsibility."

I stood up. "Do you think I want to be a Slayer? Look at me! I'm afraid of, well, everything, I freeze under pressure and my only Slaying skill appears to be menstrual cramps. But it's who I am now. It sucks, but that's the way it is. Colby never asked for the whole Protector gig, which has caused her nothing but problems, but it's who she is. You think the full-bloods will thank her for risking everything and saving them from demon possessions? No, they'll insist she's still going to fulfill the Prophesy and end their existence in some other way."

He grew agitated. "Do you think because two girls accept their lot in life, that will shame me into accepting mine?"

I stood up to him. "No, I think it's time to stop feeling sorry for yourself and suck it up."

Instead of getting angry like I expected, he gave me a hint of a smile. "You're a bossy little thing, you know that?"

I dropped down to my knees in front of him. "I can't do this without you, Hunter."

He leaned forward and kissed me tenderly on the lips. "You won't ever have to, I promise."

He wrapped his arms around me and we kissed some more. He was such a great kisser. He made me feel complete. I hoped Colby was getting a similar treatment from Thomas when a thought struck me. I pulled away.

"Ohmigod! The Prophesy! That didn't even occur to me. Come on, we've to get to Psi Phi House." I jumped up and pulled Hunter to his feet.

"We have to go *now*?" He couldn't believe it.

"Yes, yes. I've just figured it out. Come on."

We made it to Psi Phi House in record time. Thomas and Colby were sitting together on the couch, completely oblivious to anything going on around them. They were so into each other. Ahh, that was nice. But I had something important to share.

"I figured out the Prophesy," I announced, plopping down across from them.

Hunter stood awkwardly, staring at Thomas. "Hunter, this is Thomas. Thomas, this is Hunter. He's a Demon Slayer."

Thomas stood up and offered Hunter his hand. For a moment I worried Hunter couldn't bring himself to accept it but he did.

"Colby told me all about your new status, Piper. That's pretty amazing," he said to me.

"No more amazing than you two. Want to know why?"

They exchanged a look.

"Well?" Colby prompted.

"We know Colby is the one in the Prophesy. The first two lines—'*This time the mixed blood will rise, The One who is Undead but Alive*'—that's Colby. But the second part is not Colby. '*Who is pure but not whole*' doesn't mean her at all. It means Thomas. He is a vampire who is pure in intention but not whole, because he is missing part of his soul. Get it?"

They both stared at me in confusion.

"Don't you see? Only when you two fused together and became soul mates did you save Thomas, not only from demon possession but from all those other annoying vampire maladies that plague older Undead, such as paranoia, isolationism and flat-out craziness. Those were all caused by having a hole in the soul.

"'*And they will bring forth the beginning of the end*' means you two showed the way. Half-bloods who bond with full-bloods can save the vampire race by filling the missing pieces in their essences. No more nutso older vampires who go rogue, become possessed by demons and try to knock each other off. They keep their humanity, therefore staying sane."

It was like a lightbulb went off over both of their heads.

"I can't believe it! I think you're right, Piper!" Colby exclaimed. "I think that must be it. The beginning of the end doesn't refer to the beginning of the end of the world, but the beginning of a new era for vampires, ending the old ways."

Thomas nodded. "You might have it right, Piper. But will they believe it? Change is difficult for us. Will other vampires accept this new interpretation of the Prophesy?"

Colby chimed in, "If Mr. Holloway includes this interpretation in the vampire bulletin then we've got a shot. It's more likely to be believed coming from the Tribunal."

Thomas looked at me with something akin to awe. "Not bad, Slayer. Not bad at all."

There was a ruckus at the front door. It sounded like a cat, mewling at the top of its lungs. I jumped up to answer the door.

"You've got to be kidding me. I didn't even ask them yet," I said to the gray cat.

"This is nice, real nice." The cat nodded in approval. "I'm gonna like it here."

"Piper, who's at the door?" Colby asked.

"It's, well, it's—"

"Fluffy?" Hunter asked.

"Hunter! Long time. Glad to see you made it through the action. Was worried about ya. Mr. Whiskers filled me in on the details. You got one heck of a gal on your hands," Fluffy said.

"Piper?" Colby asked uncertainly.

I wasn't sure what to do. Technically, Fluffy helped in the demon defeat but I was in no position to give him a home at Psi Phi House.

"You see, Colby, Fluffy told me all about the Avarice Demons at Mrs. Murphy's and even warned me about the plot to get Aunt Chloe. That's why I called Animal Control on them. He wanted, well, he's looking for a new home and wants—"

"Oh, no, not here. You know I'm allergic."

"I know that. I told him I'd see what I could do. I swear I didn't promise him a home, just that I would ask you." I looked helplessly over at Hunter, who raised his hands, indicating he wasn't going to get sucked into this one.

"That's a fine how-do-you-do. After what I did for you?" The cat circled me.

"Listen, I'm sorry. But she's allergic to cats."

Sophie made her way downstairs in time to see the cat in the living room. "Oh, miss!" she cried. "Did you change your mind? Is this our new pet?" She rushed over and scooped Fluffy into her arms, stroking his fur and making kissy noises at him.

Colby and Thomas exchanged a look.

"I think this dame likes me," the cat purred.

"Miss?" Sophie asked, her bright eyes shining.

Colby looked at Sophie, the cat and then me, her eyes narrowing. "You owe me. Big-time.

"Fine, Fluffy can stay but he lives in your room, Sophie. I don't want cat hair on everything. I'll just take allergy medicine if I need to," she finished lamely.

Sophie squealed in delight, taking Fluffy straight upstairs. Thomas hugged Colby. "It won't be that bad, I promise."

"Oh, I know it won't," she said smugly, looking at me with calculating eyes. "Because Piper is going to move in here and make sure of it. Aren't you, Piper?"

"But why do I have to?" I choked.

Colby smiled in satisfaction. "Because you're a Demon Slayer, Piper, and he's a demon. You've got my back, right?"

I looked helplessly at Hunter, then at Colby. "Fine, I'll move in, but I'm not playing Dr. Dolittle and reciting everything he says to Sophie."

But we all knew I would.

Author's Note

But what about Carl? You send him off to New York City and then what? Nothing? Never fear, dear reader, Carl is Undead and well in an upcoming anthology with Julie Kenner and Johanna Edwards entitled *Fendi, Ferragamo, and Fangs*, a July 2007 Berkley Jam release.

Carl holds a special place in my heart and since I knew I was hooking Piper up with Hunter in *Dating-4Demons*, I wanted to give Carl his own story and the romance he deserved. I think you'll find Sydney is a perfect match for him. And you thought I'd leave you hangin'? Sheesh.

Enjoy the bite!

—Serena Robar